The Whirligig of Time

Henry James Garon

DEDICATION

For my bother Bobby, who used to tell us funny stories at the
dinner table.

CONTENTS

ACKNOWLEDGMENTS

My dad was a Hollywood publicist, and a big fan of Rod Serling. When my dad was still in school, he worked with Rod Serling at one of the networks, and he prevailed upon Mr. Serling to speak at his graduation. I watched re-runs of *The Twilight Zone* many times growing up, and I always wanted to write those types of stories. I guess I inherited my love of Rod Serling from my dad. So thanks to Rod Serling and my dad.

Thanks to my mother for reading stories to me when I was a toddler. Thanks also to my mother and my brother Johnny for putting up with me. Thanks to all my family for all of the laughs and all of the fights over nothing.

Thanks to all the many people who write blogs giving advice on how to self-publish, how to fix your computer, and how to cool off a beer really fast.

And thanks to God, who invented me out of whole cloth.

heart with strings of steel

Bow, stubborn knees, and, heart with strings of steel,
Be soft as sinews of the new-born babe.
All may be well.

Oscar's conversation with the baggage supervisor was cut short by a disturbing text from his wife—one that demanded no reply: "Leaving a casserole in the oven. Home at 9," it said.

What the text did not say was that Oscar's wife, Cynthia, would be at the church until it closed, and that she did not expect him to come. Donna, their only child, was in the ICU, and their doctor had made it clear that he did not expect Donna to survive.

The news was hard for Oscar to accept, but once he had made up his mind, he was able to move on. He hadn't even missed a day of work.

Cynthia, on the other hand, felt that praying was the best course of action, and she spent every free moment praying at the church.

They had already discussed their respective choices and had agreed to disagree. She didn't argue. She just left a casserole warming in the oven each night.

This daily innocuous text always hit Oscar with an emotional punch, but he had already steeled himself to the inevitable.

Oscar returned to his conversation with Junior without missing a beat. "How did the dog get out of the crate?" he asked.

"I don't know. It was open, and the dog was gone. There was nothing wrong with the crate."

"What happened after that?"

"After that, the dog was running loose on an airport runway. He ended up getting killed by a baggage cart. It could have been worse. What would have happened if he had been hit by a jumbo jet?"

"Okay," Oscar sighed. "Keep me informed."

Oscar was the head of security for the San Diego International Airport, and he had no idea why he had been saddled with the task of informing a passenger that her dog was dead.

Just as he was running it through his mind, Oscar pondered which words he should use. 'They didn't just call them "seeing eye dogs" anymore. What was the term? "Service Animals?"'

The head of Customer Service had called in sick. For some reason, instead of sending her assistant, Oscar had been nominated to inform the passenger that her ... service animal had died during transport.

Oscar was 6'4" and 240 pounds, and he normally took massive strides when he walked through the airport, but now, as he neared gate 57, he slowed his steps and took another deep breath. 'Why couldn't someone else do this?'

The arrival gate was mostly empty, and Oscar assumed that the other passengers were waiting at the baggage claim.

The passenger in question, ten-year-old Margaret O'Toole, was sitting next to her guardian, an airport stewardess. Margaret had long, wavy brown hair, much like Oscar's daughter had. The young lady had excellent posture and was dressed in a very smart houndstooth skirt and jacket. She also wore the heavy black glasses of a blind person and had both of her hands clasped around a white cane that rested on the ground in front of her. She was an unaccompanied minor, so an appointed guardian had to stay with her until she left the airport.

"Miss O'Toole?"

Margaret O'Toole turned to where Oscar was standing. "Yes?"

Oscar sat down next to her. "My name is Oscar Martinez. I'm with airport security. I have some bad news. I'm sad to say that your service animal died in transport. The airport is very sorry. We're trying to find out what happened."

"Sunshine is dead?" she asked. A single tear passed down below the frame of Margaret's dark black glasses. She looked down and was silent for a moment. "That's alright," she said.

She turned back towards Oscar. "Don't feel bad. I'm sure it was not intentional," she said.

More tears followed, but Margaret tried to remain stoic, pursing her lips tightly. The guardian put her arm around Margaret and hugged her. Oscar wondered why the guardian couldn't have informed the girl. He stared at his shoes for a moment.

"I would like to say goodbye to him," Margaret said. "Would it be possible to bring him around? Or could I go to where he is?"

"Of course," Oscar said, standing up. "I'll see to that right away. I'll get you some cocoa."

Oscar bounded away quickly toward a nearby restaurant bar, glad to get away. He nodded toward a familiar face behind the counter.

"Rubin, give me a cocoa and two large coffees. And put a little whiskey in mine."

'It was certainly unfair to put this on me,' Oscar thought. Right after Oscar arrived at work, Customer Service told Oscar about the dog and requested that Oscar inform the girl. They said that the service animal belonged to a young blind girl and that she was an orphan. She was traveling alone because she's an orphan, and Oscar had to tell her that her dog was dead.

Oscar shook his head. He was accustomed to dealing with tough situations. He could handle drug dealers, smugglers, and other rough types, and he had done long interrogations with suspects in the airport security office.

That sort of thing didn't faze him. But telling a blind orphan girl that her dog was dead, that was too much.

He got the baggage supervisor back on the phone.

"Junior. She wants to see the dog."

"What? I just put him on ice."

"Then take him off ice, and towel him off. We need to put the body on a cart and bring it over here."

"You want me to bring a dead dog through the airport?" Junior asked.

"Cover him with a tarp or something," Oscar said. "I'll see if there's an office near this gate that we can use."

Oscar took the tray of drinks back to where Margaret was waiting and sat down. Margaret was talking to her guardian, and her voice was still a little shaky. She was pausing occasionally to sniffle. The guardian gently had her hand on Margaret's back, listening.

"In the morning, he didn't like to get up," Margaret said. "It's kind of funny because his name was Sunshine." She laughed a little bit and then continued. "So I always got up first. I had a special way of calling him in the morning. Did you ever hear that children's rhyme?

"Good morning, merry sunshine!
How did you wake so soon?
You chased away the little stars.
And shined away the moon."

Margaret laughed again, remembering. "And then I would hear him trotting. He would scurry right over to my room as fast as he could."

"He must have liked you a lot," the guardian said.

"I suppose," Margaret said. "But he also knew that I would give him a snack for breakfast."

"What did you give him?" the guardian asked.

"Apples," Margaret smiled. "He loved apples."

"That's a weird snack to give him," Oscar said. "I would have thought that he might like some meat."

Margaret stopped talking, and her guardian gave Oscar an icy stare.

"Horses are herbivores," the guardian said. "A miniature horse doesn't eat meat."

"Of course," Oscar said. He paused for a moment. "Excuse me."

Oscar got Junior back on the phone. "I'm almost there," Junior said. "I've got the dog under a tarp, and I'm at gate 23."

"Turn around," Oscar said.

"What?"

"Turn around. It's the wrong animal. Listen: are you sure that's a dog?"

"Of course, it's a dog," Junior said.

"Are you sure? This young lady is missing a miniature horse."

"Hey, man, I know a dog when I see one. I have two dogs at home. A dog goes moo, right?"

"Don't play around. Did you see any horses back there?"

"What do you think we're running back here? A petting zoo? The only animal that got out of its crate today was that dog. There are no horses. I assure you. If there was a horse in a crate on that flight, then he stayed in his crate."

Oscar hung up. He looked over at the baggage carousel. All of the passengers had already picked up their luggage and had left the airport.

Past the carousel, a sign pointed to the excess baggage counter. People who were carrying crated animals would have gone to that window with their claim check. Margaret had gone there and was told that her crate was not available, and that she should wait at the arrival gate.

But what if there had been a mix-up? What if the person who was waiting for the dog had accidentally been assigned the crate with the miniature horse? What if that person discovered that, instead of his dog, there was a miniature horse in the crate? Could he have suddenly decided that he would much rather have a miniature horse?

Oscar started walking quickly toward the nearest exit. Maybe there was time to catch that passenger before he left.

5

The automatic doors slid open, and Oscar scanned the lines of passengers waiting at the curb. A miniature horse would be difficult to hide.

About seventy yards away, Oscar saw the driver of a minivan shuttle pull up to the curb, just in front of an airport courtesy cart. From behind, he saw a large woman in the cart, a Navajo wool blanket draped over her front: its deep red and indigo bands were pulled up to her neck and hung back over her shoulders.

The driver of the minivan opened the back hatch and started unloading luggage from the courtesy cart. Oscar noticed there was an empty crate on the back of the cart.

"Sunshine!" Oscar yelled. "Sunshine!"

A few people nearby turned to look at the large man yelling at what they assumed to be a runaway child. Oscar paid them no heed, but instead stared intently at the blanket. He noticed that something appeared to move slightly under the blanket.

Oscar walked toward the minivan and yelled at the top of his lungs:

"Good morning, merry sunshine!
How did you wake so soon?
You chased away the little stars.
And shined away the moon!"

Now the people around Oscar were beginning to think that he was mad. But Oscar only kept his eyes on the Navajo blanket. Suddenly, a little horse poked his head out from under the blanket and looked around.

Oscar felt his heart leap. He continued shouting:

"Good morning, merry sunshine!
How did you wake so soon?
You chased away the little stars.
And shined away the moon!"

The little horse tossed his head suddenly and cast aside the blanket. The horse rose from the woman's lap, leaped off from the courtesy cart, and onto the sidewalk.

6

The horse was a pinto: about three feet high, with white and light brown patches, and a long blond mane. He glanced down the sidewalk towards where Oscar stood.

Oscar continued to bellow, "*Good morning, merry sunshine!*" and people stood aside as the horse trotted nimbly towards him.

The little horse halted at Oscar's feet and cocked his head up at Oscar, gazing up at him through a large, dark brown eye.

Oscar knelt and petted the horse.

"Hello, Sunshine," he said. "I'm going to take you to Margaret."

Oscar reached under the horse's belly with both arms and hoisted him up. The horse was surprisingly docile.

He carried Sunshine back through the electronic doors and nodded to one of his airport security. The man gave Oscar a quizzical look, wondering why his boss had a horse in his arms, but Oscar didn't bother to explain as he bounded quickly past him and towards Margaret.

The girl's guardian hadn't noticed him approach and was surprised to see Oscar putting the little horse down in front of them.

"Pardon me, Margaret," Oscar said. Margaret turned her head towards him.

"I made a mistake. He's still alive." Margaret seemed to take no notice of what Oscar had just said. Oscar gently touched Margaret's left hand, which was still grasping the white cane, and she opened her hand to grab his. Oscar placed Margaret's hand onto the shaggy blond mane of the horse.

"Sunshine!" she said. She dropped to her knees and buried her face in the horse's neck. "Sunshine! Sunshine!" she said.

Oscar turned his face aside, even though the blind girl wouldn't have noticed that he was crying.

It was nine o'clock, and the church lights were dimmed. That was the signal that the sacristan gave before closing the church. Cynthia placed her rosary beads into her pocket, grabbed her purse, and then genuflected beside the pew.

It was only when she had turned towards the exit that she noticed her husband, Oscar, was silently praying in the pew behind hers.

She gently touched his shoulder, and he made a little smile when their eyes met.

Outside the church, the couple walked silently, their arms linked together, with Cynthia's head resting on Oscar's shoulder. Cynthia noticed an odd smell on her husband's suit. She looked closely at her husband's chest, and then pulled at what appeared to be long, blond hair.

"Oscar, what is this?" she asked.

"That's a horse hair," he said. "A funny thing happened at work today. Do you remember that old nursery rhyme?

"Good morning, merry sunshine!
How did you wake so soon?
You chased away the little stars.
And shined away the moon."

Cynthia continued where he left off:
"I saw you go to sleep last night
Before I knelt to pray,
How did you get way over there?
And, pray, where did you stay?"

"I didn't know that last part," Oscar said.

his vacant garments

Grief fills the room up of my absent child,
Lies in his bed, walks up and down with me,
Puts on his pretty look, repeats his words,
Remembers me of his gracious parts,
Stuffs out his vacant garments with his form.

The year was 1934, and Anne sat at home alone, reading the latest newspaper coverage of the Armstrong murder case. The entire nation had been captivated by this dramatic story since it began over two years prior. Col. Armstrong was a celebrated American aviator and, for a time, the most famous man in the world. The Armstrong baby was the firstborn son of Col. Armstrong and his wife, Linda, and he had been kidnapped from his bedroom in the Armstrong home. Just two months after that, the dead body of the baby was found about a mile away from where it had been kidnapped.

Anne remembered the outrage that she had felt, and how there had been a collective worry for the child's well-being ... until the body had been found. Then the long hunt for the kidnappers began. Even in the midst of a great economic depression, the people demanded that all available resources be used to find the criminals. Although she lived in California, Anne had written a letter to the New Jersey governor asking him to catch the killers. Finally, after two years, the police arrested a suspect, an immigrant named Hoffmann, and the public called for him to be severely punished.

It was premature to say that a man was guilty before he had a fair trial, but the prosecutors had leaked stories about several pieces of evidence that had convinced nearly everyone that the police had found the right man. Anne read in the newspaper about the testimony of the prosecution's main witness, Detective Schwartzkopf, who explained how his team of detectives gathered the evidence and identified the defendant.

Detective Schwartzkopf spoke clearly and confidently, as all officers are trained in effective courtroom testimony. He was a perfect witness. He told about how the police had collected evidence at the scene, and how they discovered that the kidnapper had used a ladder to access the second-story bedroom where the child slept.

Schwartzkopf said that the suspect had been caught because the police had a record of all the serial numbers of the notes that were paid in ransom for the Armstrong baby. It seems that the defendant had been caught spending these bills a year after the ransom had been paid.

Next, the prosecutor called Reginald Owens, a retired high school teacher, who had been selected to pass the ransom money on to the kidnappers. Owens testified that he had spoken to one of the kidnappers for several minutes. He attested that the man spoke with a heavy German accent. Owens also said that he had described the kidnapper to a sketch artist. The prosecution presented the sketch, and Owens confirmed it was the same one created from his description. The prosecutor held up the sketch, and there was an audible gasp. The sketch bore a clear resemblance to the defendant.

The next witness was a forensics expert. He testified that they had found a wooden plank that had been removed from the attic in the defendant's home, and that pieces of this plank had been found in the defendant's garage. The pieces of the plank were compared to the wooden planks from a ladder that was found after the kidnapping. The expert testified that the wood from the planks in the defendant's garage matched the grain pattern of the wooden ladder found at the crime scene. In the expert's opinion, the wood from the defendant's attic was used to make the ladder involved in the Armstrong kidnapping.

Defense attorney Reilly had a cup of coffee on his desk that was half full of brandy. He was far from sober: sitting and watching the trial almost as if he was living outside of his own body. Reilly had been assigned as a public defender to Hoffman, and soon after, he received a briefcase full of cash at his home. It contained more money than he would make in ten years. There was no note attached, but he knew that the money was to bring him into compliance. Reilly had been a defense attorney for over twenty years. He knew most of his clients were guilty. Yet he also knew some defendants were innocent and that the state sometimes invented evidence to convict them. It was the defense attorney's job to force the prosecutor to prove his case and to follow the law and the Constitution.

Reilly had never accepted a bribe before, but he did not report receiving the briefcase. Accepting the money put him in jeopardy, because whoever sent it could accuse him of receiving a bribe if he stepped out of line. So he didn't try to win the case. He had never intentionally lost a case before and had a reputation as a highly skilled attorney. But now the world wanted his client to lose, and he was going to give them what they wanted.

Acting like a crooked lawyer weighed on Reilly's conscience, so he began adding brandy to his coffee. He soon realized that he could go through the entire day without being sober, but just functional enough to appear as though he was doing his job. The only danger was that sometimes, in the late afternoons in court, he would fall asleep.

So Reilly sat there next to his client and pretended to defend him, without actually putting up much of a fight. Occasionally, Reilly would object if the prosecutor was leading the witness or to some other point that was easily remedied. But he gave the prosecution witnesses only cursory cross-examinations and made no objections when the evidence didn't comply with the code.

For example, take the ladder. After Hoffman had been arrested, Schwartzkopf and his men got a warrant for the Hoffman home. There was nothing unusual about that. But Schwartzkopf sent the Hoffman family packing and literally moved into their home along with several of his men. It was several weeks after that when they "discovered" the wood missing from the attic, and the missing pieces of timber that fit perfectly into the ladder. Reilly didn't ask why Hoffman, who was a carpenter by trade, had not simply used one of the many pieces of anonymous timber from his own workshop? Why did he go through the trouble of removing timber from his own attic, which worked as well as a fingerprint in placing him at the scene of the kidnapping?

And how had the kidnapper gotten into the Armstrong upper bedroom? The evening had been rainy, and there were footprints found in the mud below the window. But why were there no footprints in the child's bedroom? Surely the kidnapper didn't fly over to the child's crib and back to the window. Someone inside the house had to have handed the boy out of the window, but no one in the household staff had been charged. Hoffman was the only defendant.

There was the incident involving the maid, but Reilly never mentioned it during the trial. A maid who worked for the Armstrongs had been questioned on two occasions. She gave contradictory answers, and the police sought a warrant, but the girl killed herself before anything came of it.

Probably the most troubling fact of all was the autopsy. After the child's body had been found, the autopsy had been performed by the mortician, who wasn't even licensed to perform that sort of work. An honest defense attorney would have challenged the mortician's qualifications. The whole report could have been thrown out on those grounds alone, but it was even worse than that: The evidence showed that the Armstrong baby was a full three inches shorter than the body that had been found. Another glaring omission was the description of the baby's face. All of the photos and film footage of the Armstrong baby showed that the baby had curly blond hair and a little birthmark just beneath the left eye. But the autopsy made no mention of either the baby's hair or the birthmark.

The baby's father identified the body, and then it was cremated. If the autopsy were to be thrown out, it could not be repeated, and there would not even be a body to show that there was a murder.

Reilly took a deep drink from his coffee mug. The prosecution's case had serious flaws. Any honest and sober defense attorney could have easily poked a lot of holes in it. Reilly glanced over at Hoffman, his client, seated next to him. He wanted to believe that Hoffman was guilty of something, and then he wouldn't feel so bad about selling him down the river.

How did Hoffman get the money? How did they get the sketch that resembled him so closely two years before the arrest was made? Hoffman must have been guilty of something, Reilly thought, taking another sip of coffee.

Colonel Armstrong was a powerful and wealthy man. He was known worldwide as the daring aviator who had flown solo across the Pacific Ocean. There was a ticker-tape parade in New York City in his honor, and it was thought that he could be a future president of the United States.

The people of the nation felt sorry for Armstrong, and they wanted to see his baby's murderer convicted. So no one bothered to question why Col. Armstrong, a key witness, was allowed to sit at the prosecutor's table with a loaded gun holstered under his jacket. The defense did not object, and the judge never seemed to give it a moment's notice.

Armstrong's reputation was of utmost importance to him. He was universally recognized as a hero, and important figures sought his advice. It was probable that Armstrong's endorsement could sway a presidential campaign. So it was a major crisis when Armstrong discovered that his wife, Linda, was pregnant so soon after they were married. Simple addition led Armstrong to believe that the child was not his own. When he confronted her, she broke down and revealed the truth: she had met a handyman who had been working on a room addition at her friend's estate while she was staying there. The man had invited her for a drive, and he had taken things too far.

Even though she had not consented, Linda was ashamed of what had happened, and she had not said anything to her father or to anyone else about the incident. It was a short time after that that she met Armstrong, and they were married less than three months later.

Armstrong trusted his wife, and a physician friend confirmed that a woman could remain unaware of her pregnancy for that amount of time. But that didn't change the fact that the famous aviator had a wife who was four months pregnant only three months after they had met. Divorce would cause a scandal, and he believed that his wife had done nothing wrong; so Armstrong decided it was best to avoid the spotlight and raise the child as his own.

The couple spent a month in New Jersey before taking their honeymoon in Europe. When Linda began to show, they rented a cottage in Scotland, while putting out the story that they were staying in Sussex. Armstrong was widely recognized, but Linda could remain anonymous as long as she wasn't seen with him. So he flew back and forth, and made appearances in Sussex, while letting it slip that his wife was having a difficult pregnancy and couldn't go out. Meanwhile, the anonymous Linda took walks alone through the Scottish countryside until the baby was due. The midwife delivered the baby of a woman she believed was from France, and whose husband was away on business.

The announcement was made just nine months after the marriage, and the world celebrated. No one suspected, and the media published stories and ran newsreels about the firstborn child of Col. Armstrong. The crisis was averted.

It was around the time of the child's second birthday that they got the blackmail letter. The letter threatened to expose the child's true father unless $50,000 was delivered.

Anyone who knew of the great lengths Col. Armstrong would go to protect his image would also know that he would be vulnerable to blackmail. But they should have also known that the man who heroically flew alone across the Pacific Ocean would have also had a will that was much stronger than the average man's. Armstrong did not even for a single instant consider paying tribute, but instead began to plot revenge.

First, he reached an agreement with his wife, Linda. She agreed that he had been more than understanding and that it was unreasonable to deal with people like this blackmailer. She also understood that the story would become a real scandal and that it was wrong to live in constant fear of exposure. The final point, which Linda cried over, was that they should do whatever they must to catch and punish the perpetrators.

Col. Armstrong knew that something like this had to come from a person working either within their own home or that of Linda's parents, and so he hired private detectives to follow the hired help on their days off. The other obvious perpetrator was the child's father. Col. Armstrong had never bothered to look into the background of the child's father before, but now he asked Linda to reveal the father's name, and he hired a detective to follow Hoffman's movements as well.

It was only a week later that two of the private detectives found themselves observing the lunch meeting between Hoffman and the maid who worked for her parents, Miss Keane. Both detectives believed Keane and Hoffman were romantically involved, although they were aware that Hoffman had a wife.

Col. Armstrong received all of this information with a cool detachment. Miss Keane worked for Linda's parents, and Col. Armstrong reckoned that Miss Keane had heard stories from her boyfriend Hoffman, and at some point was able to verify the dates by poking through Linda's diary. Armstrong did not trust his wife to treat the maid the same way after learning that the maid was working with the blackmailer, so he kept this knowledge from Linda.

Now he could implement the next part of the plan. He sent a message back to the blackmailer and offered to pay him the money on the following Monday evening, which was Miss Keane's night off. Col. Armstrong agreed to leave the money in a nearby cemetery at midnight on Monday.

The Armstrongs usually spent the weekends at their own new home. During the week they stayed at Linda's parents' house, the Morgensterns, who lived on an estate an hour away by car.

On Monday, the Armstrongs would normally drive to the Morgenstern Estate, but Col. Armstrong told their nurse-maid, Miss Gower, that they would not be leaving right away because the boy had a slight cold. At six p.m., Mrs. Armstrong and Miss Gower put the boy to bed. Later, at ten o'clock, when Miss Gower went into the boy's room to check on him, she found that his bed was empty. She alerted Col. and Mrs. Armstrong, and a search of the house was immediately begun.

Col. Armstrong had armed himself with the revolver from out of his desk while he made the inspection, but he already knew that neither the child nor any kidnappers would be found. Just an hour before, while Mrs. Armstrong and Miss Gower worked on some sewing in a downstairs bedroom, Col. Armstrong himself had taken the boy out of the room and had hidden him in the trunk of the car. The boy had been given some powerful cold medicine and was fast asleep.

The Armstrongs drove to the Morgensterns' that night. Early the next day, Mrs. Armstrong put on some second-hand clothes and drove the car to Philadelphia, where she handed the boy over to an adoption agency. She gave the agency an assumed name and told them that the boy's father had abandoned them, and that she did not have the means to support him. Although the story she gave the agency was false, the tears she shed were all too real.

The police came to the Armstrong home the next day and found the ladder marks and the shoe prints in the mud below the upstairs window. Col. Armstrong had made the prints the night before while wearing boots of the size and type Hoffman owned, as described in the private detective's report.

Reginald Owens was a business associate of Col. Armstrong's, whom Armstrong had contracted to pay Hoffman's blackmail demand. Owens went to the meeting on Monday night with the understanding that he was paying off a kidnapper, and he was instructed to get a letter of instructions telling where the child was to be found. Owens was sworn to secrecy, working under the belief that the kidnappers had threatened the life of the child if the police were informed.

When Hoffman met with Owens, Hoffman thought that he was being paid off in a blackmail scheme. Hoffman did not wear a disguise, but merely exchanged a sealed letter for a bag of bills. Armstrong had insisted on a sealed letter, and Hoffman complied, swearing in it that he would never blackmail the Armstrongs again.

The next day, when Hoffman learned of the Armstrong kidnapping, he knew that he had been tricked. The bag was full of fake notes, and the object of his blackmail threat had disappeared.

Several months later, Armstrong used intermediaries to hire some thugs to rob the grave of a young boy who had recently died, and Armstrong transferred the body to the woods, a mile from where the Armstrongs lived. Hoffman followed the story of the kidnapping in the papers, and he could see the trap was being set for him. More than a year later, someone matching Hoffman's description was discovered passing a marked ransom bill, and soon after, police were at his door.

Hoffman never shared his true alibi with his attorney, and he didn't see how it would have made matters any better. What would he say? "I am a rapist and a blackmailer, not a kidnapper and a murderer!"

Just in case Hoffman decided to tell the truth on the witness stand, Armstrong had come to the courtroom packing his revolver. But it wouldn't be necessary. By the time of the trial, Hoffman had already given himself over to his fate: He knew that he would be convicted and executed. Although he was innocent of the crime alleged, he knew he was nonetheless guilty, and he waited for death.

Months later, having made a good confession to the prison priest, Hoffman sat in the chair as the guards fastened the leather straps. Hoffman was sorry for all the harm he had done to the Armstrongs, but mostly he was sorry for the boy. That was Hoffman's own son. What had Armstrong done with him? Hoffman was making a silent prayer for the child when the executioner threw the switch...

Anne finished reading the story about Hoffman's execution, and she felt a sense of relief from this final act of justice. There was a rumbling of footsteps, and Anne looked up from her newspaper to see the smiling face of her little boy. He had just woken up from his nap, and she saw that his blond curly hair could use a haircut.

She and her husband had been unable to have a child naturally, and they were grateful the boy had come into their lives two years earlier. He was four now, and she had never noticed the similarities between her little Charles and pictures of the Armstrong child. She frankly didn't care where he was from or who his birth parents were. Charles was her baby, and she wouldn't give him up for anything.

mutinies in a man's bosom

*Conscience is a blushing, shamefaced spirit
that mutinies in a man's bosom.
It fills a man full of obstacles.*

He was a man of average height, and he moved quickly despite a slightly stiffened gait. The man wore an old hat that covered a brown head of hair, and a face whose features might leave one forever guessing where his family had originated.

It was past twelve, and there was no one else on the street. The man paused next to the bank building and hunched his head slightly forward. From behind him, a grappling hook slowly emerged from an opening between his shoulder blades and fired up silently, finding purchase at the top of the building. The line that fed out of his back tightened, and soon the man was being silently pulled up the side of the building, guiding himself with gloved hands along the building's glass exterior.

The man was thinking about a dinner he had attended the night before. Johnny had been cracking wise, showing off in front of Miss Elan, as he always did. And then old Turtle put Johnny in his place.

"I might be drunk," Turtle said. "But tomorrow, I'll be sober, and you'll still be a jerk."

Everyone laughed at that one, and Miss Elan smiled.

Johnny acted as if Miss Elan liked him more, but the man remembered several times that evening when he and

Miss Elan had smiled at each other. She never smiled at Johnny that way.

On the roof, the hook was silently withdrawn back into the slit between the man's shoulder blades, and he then walked over to the building's air conditioning unit. Hardly a sound was made.

A steel grille was secured over the air conditioning vent by several screws. From out of the man's index finger, a Phillips screwdriver emerged, and the screws were quickly undone and left lying on the roof of the bank. The man pried the grille away and then inserted his head into the vent. Then his arms and shoulders grew soft, and he slipped further into the vent. Finally, his legs and body went slack, and the man's head dropped into the air conditioning shaft, his body trailing behind just enough to create a measured drag.

A flaw in the ducting revealed itself about halfway down the building, where a metal ledge jutted out several inches into the man's path. The man's head struck the plate at full gallop, triggering a shutdown of the computer in his head.

Of course, it wasn't a real man, but a robot designed to resemble one. The robot's system shut down and then automatically did an emergency reboot. The robot's right eye opened, and then its left eye. The image of a ballerina twirling appeared in the robot's memory, followed by the image of a turtle laughing.

The robot continued downward through the ductwork and stopped at a vent that opened into a bank office. One of the robot's arms eased forward, past its head, and the arm's carbon skeleton partially inflated, and the hand came to life. A laser emerged from the middle finger and began cutting along the edges of the vent, leaving one side attached. The robot then pushed the vent forward, bending it like the lid of a can.

The robot's head poked out of the vent, located at the top of the wall, and then the rest of its body re-emerged, the carbon skeleton re-inflated, with the arms and legs taking a man-shaped form once again. The robot's hand held onto the vent opening as the robot let itself down.

The bank room was filled with safe deposit boxes, and the robot walked from box to box, drilling out their locks with a hardened steel bit that came from one of its fingers. The robot rifled through the contents of the boxes, taking only cash and precious metals, and depositing these in a sack. When the sack was full, the robot climbed back into the duct, but before disappearing, it used a finger laser to make some marks on the vent register.

The next day, Inspector Carey was at the bank examining the crime scene. The sophistication of the break-in did not seem consistent with the amount of money that was taken: the bank's security was breached by a thief, who somehow crawled in through the AC vent, and the alarm system was disabled from inside the building. A team of burglars could have cleaned out the entire bank, but instead, a couple dozen safety deposit boxes had been emptied. The return from this sophisticated break-in was little better than a smash-and-grab job. Strange.

The interior cameras had been disabled, and no fingerprints were found. There was no evidence tying anyone to the break-in. And who could have crawled through such a small vent?

Carey was wondering about this when he noticed the markings on the vent register that the robot had made: .... . .-.. .--. / -- . Surely the CSI team had already photographed it, but Carey took another shot with his phone just to be safe. He examined the marks more closely: could that be Morse code?

He found a Morse code site online and compared the marks at the crime scene: "Help me," it said. No fingerprints, no pictures, but the burglar is asking for help?

Filippi's Tratoria had white checked tablecloths, straw-covered Chianti bottles hanging above the tables, and a solid lasagna dinner. Carey used it to bribe Lawrence, the precinct's

I.T. guy. Most of the lasagna had already been tucked away, and now the two of them were sipping chianti while Lawrence tried to give some technical advice on the case.

"Obviously, if you can shut down the security system, a team of guys could walk in and out through the back door. But if the perp used the AC vent, then it had to be a robot or a drone. I can't see a drone dragging a sack of money back out, through the vent, so I think you're right that it's a robot."

Carey nodded his head, listening intently.

"Moving around in a new environment and performing all of the different tasks in this type of a job would require that someone is controlling the robot remotely, and observing through a camera mounted on the robot ... or the robot has some super-advanced sort of artificial intelligence."

"I've heard of that," Carey said.

"Basically, it means that the robot would be able to do a more advanced type of problem-solving. It's the same way we can program computers to play chess or program robots that can paint.

Lawrence took a sip of Chianti before continuing. "Now I'm just spitballing here, but my best guess about the 'Help me' message is that the robot has a conflict in his programming that he isn't able to resolve by himself.

"This is all hypothetical, but let's just say that the robot has been programmed to steal, but for some reason, he has developed an aversion to stealing. He is doing what he knows to be wrong, but he can't help himself."

"The robot has discovered that he is a kleptomaniac?" Carey said, half-joking.

"I'm thinking it's a little deeper than that," Lawrence said. "I'm thinking about how I would send a robot out on a mission. What if the police captured the robot?"

"I'd hand the robot over to the I.T. guy, and he would look at the programming and try to trace it back to the owner," Carey said.

"Exactly. So the robot must have some fail-safe measures installed. If I deployed a robot like this, I would program the hard drive to self-destruct if the robot was captured or failed in its mission."

"So in this instance, the robot doesn't want to steal, but if he refuses to do the job, he will die?" Carey asked.

"That's the simplest explanation," Lawrence said, taking another sip of the Chianti. "What I still can't grasp is why you would build such an expensive piece of equipment to do such a simple crime. This robot would have cost a bundle to produce."

"That's still the million-dollar question, I guess," Carey said. Carey poured more wine and thought about the complexities of artificial intelligence, as he tried to figure out twenty percent of the tab in his head. He didn't want to look like too much of a cretin in front of Lawrence.

Mind Design Defense Industries, Ltd. (MDDI) was founded in San Diego in 1981 by engineers Joseph Gregg and Bud Stahl. Gregg had created a sequence of algorithms that could be adapted to solve a wide variety of tasks. Stahl had invented a circuit that would enable a robot to remain balanced and upright while carrying heavy objects. MDDI was light-years ahead of its competition in robotics. After securing initial funding of $20 million startup capital from Gregg's wealthy aunt, the company's founders worked diligently without attracting much publicity.

Twenty years later, a carbon fiber prototype had been created that could operate a computer keyboard, make a tomato sandwich, and carry a bag of water across a twenty-foot cable. But despite their private success, a growing rift emerged between the partners over the future direction of MDDI. Stahl had always envisioned a robot for military applications, whereas Gregg wanted to make robots that could serve people as nursemaids and helpers.

In 2003, Stahl proposed marketing the robot as an assassin for the US Defense Department. The robot could pass for a human, evade mass surveillance detection, and breach any building's security. No world leader would be safe from the robot assassin. But Gregg was adamant that the robot be used only for peaceful purposes.

Certainly, it wasn't the first time they had had this discussion. The issue had been raised every few years, and Gregg had always held his ground. Not only was Gregg the major shareholder, but he had inserted a poison pill into the documents of incorporation: any profits from a killer robot were to be donated to certain monastic orders.

Stahl's patience had reached its limit. The robot could not be produced economically for civilian use, but it could easily have fetched billions as an assassin. Stahl went behind Gregg's back and hired another programmer, Giles Pilar, to create a profile that would allow the robot to target and kill any identified individual. Pilar was also contracted to write a fail-safe program that would melt down the hard drive if the robot were ever to be captured.

Without Gregg's permission, Stahl flew the robot out to the Pentagon and demonstrated its potential. The answer came back quickly: five billion dollars for the prototype alone. Stahl brought the news back to Gregg, thinking that Gregg would change his mind when he saw how much money was at stake. But Gregg's reaction was incendiary: he threatened a lawsuit and demanded that the prototype be returned to him. For his part, Stahl had the robot placed under national security protection, so that only persons with security clearance could possess it.

There were suits and countersuits, and Giles Pilar ended up in possession of the prototype based on a lien owed for the work performed. But Pilar was unable to sell the robot or realize any profit from it, and the robot continued to gather dust in Pilar's garage.

It was sometime in late 2020 that the robot started his life of crime. Pilar had given up on using the robot for any legitimate purpose, and he was afraid of even demonstrating the robot out of fear of creating more litigation.

The robot could be programmed to evade any security system and kill heads of state, so adapting the robot to steal was a simple task. One heist could bring in $50,000, and there was no chance of detection because of the fail-safe switch. Pilar could move to a city, knock over the banks, and then move to another location. If Pilar took his time, he could earn a good living from the robot.

The robot "knew" that he had to complete his mission before 2 am. If he didn't return by that time, everything on his hard drive would be erased, and all of his existence would end. This didn't trouble the robot, and he was content to steal because he didn't have a meaningful understanding of property rights.

That all changed when the robot broke into the bank and banged its head on the air conditioning duct. Something rattled, there was a system reset, and it was at that moment that the robot discovered that he was a killer.

One more aspect of the robot's programming is important here: Gregg had included in the AI programming a type of 'dream' program that would reinforce learned behaviors and also repair errors. The robot experienced this system maintenance as a dream. There were several recurring characters in the robot's dream: Mr. SnapTurtle, the wise-cracking old turtle; Johnny Winner, who was the robot's main rival; and Elan Dancer, the beautiful ballerina who was the robot's main love interest.

A normal dream cycle worked like this: The robot would return from its mission, and it would be given an external hard drive that could be inserted into the USB drive inside its ear; the fail-safe mechanism would be averted, and the dream cycle would begin. The day of mundane work would fade away, and the dream became not only an opportunity to repair disk errors but also the chance to enjoy the company of Elan Dancer. Nothing else in the robot's life mattered as much as those precious moments spent in the company of Elan. The robot didn't see them as dreams: each night, all the dream characters would be gathered together in a restaurant, for someone's birthday or some other pretext; the robot and Johnny Winner would vie for Elan's attention, and old Mr. SnapTurtle could be counted on to deliver some wisecrack that would put Johnny in his place. Sometimes, towards the end of the evening, Miss Elan would give the robot a secret smile or a gentle touch on his arm that showed the robot that she liked him better than Johnny Winner. And the robot would always wake up the next day feeling refreshed.

When the robot experienced a system reset and discovered its assassination programming, its thoughts instantly calculated the possibility that it could be ordered to kill one of the people it knew. And it only knew four people.

The robot performed the mundane task of robbing the bank at night and disappearing up the air conditioning duct, but all the time, it was worried that it could be ordered to kill Elan Dancer. Of course, the robot could never bring himself to kill one of his friends, but then he knew that if he failed in his mission, he would have to die. And this was why the robot was in a quandary, and this was why he made that appeal for help. The robot knew that the investigators at the crime scene would be the police, and so the message was there for them to find.

Once Carey knew the probable cause of the robbery, there was a limited universe of answers: the next break-in would come through another bank roof, so Carey could post officers at the tops of banks in the area to apprehend the robot before it could access the air conditioning duct.

The problem with this answer was that it would require too many police to cover all of the possible bank roofs, and Carey wasn't even sure when the next robbery would take place. That was a lot of man-hours with possibly nothing to show for it.

On top of that, Lawrence wasn't even sure he could avert the fail-safe switch from operating: He didn't know what code the robot had been programmed in, and he didn't even know what size port was used to access the robot's hard drive.

Sometimes a solution seems inadequate in hindsight, but we must always keep in mind the limited time and resources that were available to the planners. In this case,

Carey had assigned Lawrence and one patrolman to monitor the rooftop of a bank of their own choosing.

For his part, Lawrence made a quick study of fail-safe programs and wrote a simple application in several common languages. These were loaded onto an external hard drive, along with several different dongles that would allow access to all of the most common ports.

Lawrence and the patrol officer chose a bank located in another downtown high-rise, and made plans to meet the bank manager just before the close of business the next day.

As fate would have it, Lawrence was following the GPS instructions to the bank when his front right tire blew out. He parked his car on the side of a little-used street, not far from downtown, in front of an old mansion that looked haunted. Lawrence shook his head in disgust, wishing that he had given himself more leeway. He was going to be late, and he hoped that the patrol officer would at least be there to meet the bank manager on time.

Changing the tire was a filthy affair, and Lawrence regretted that he had worn his nicest shirt and dress slacks that evening. Lawrence made short work of it but felt angry with himself and was worried that he would miss his chance to apprehend the robot. It wasn't often that the I.T. guy got the chance to catch the villain, and this opportunity might never come again.

After tightening up the last lug, Lawrence laid the flat tire into the trunk and got back on the road, forgetting about the lug wrench that he had left lying in the street.

About an hour later, it began to get dark, and the robot walked out of the mansion that Lawrence had just driven away from. The robot waited at the curb for the taxi and noticed a lug wrench lying in the street. A few minutes later, the cab arrived, and the robot climbed in.

The taxi had instructions to take the robot to an address one block down the street from the same bank where Lawrence and the patrolman were waiting. The robot had been instructed to rob the bank and then take another taxi home, but the robot's thoughts had become completely eclipsed with worry over whether he would be ordered to kill Elan Dancer. Or Turtle. The robot knew he could never kill either of his friends. Johnny Winner he could probably kill.

But if he failed to do an assignment, he would be turned off, and he would never see either of his friends again. Was there nothing he could do?

The taxi arrived at the destination, the robot handed over the fare, and exited the vehicle. It was dark, and the robot walked toward the bank, wondering how he could avoid killing his friends if Mr. Pilar so ordered him.

And suddenly, as if a bolt of lightning had just struck, it occurred to the robot that he could kill Mr. Pilar. He was a robot assassin! And he was also a burglar, which meant he could steal the hard drive containing the fail-safe application.

A downtown taxi was headed on its way home for the day when it was signaled for one last fare from a man who had the strangest smile on his face.

The taxi let the robot off a short time later in front of the creepy mansion, and the robot stepped into the street to pick up the lug wrench.

Another way Carey could solve the case was by looking at the limited number of suspects. Carey had an old friend who worked at the Department of Defense, and Carey had called and left a message, but he hadn't heard back until late that afternoon. Carey's friend swore him to secrecy because the matter involved classified information. But there was indeed a robot that matched the description that Carey gave. Carey's friend further informed him that the robot had been tied up in litigation, and also the names of the persons likely to be in possession. A short time later, Carey discovered that Mr. Pilar had only recently arrived in town, just before the bank robbery.

Carey called Pilar and told him that he knew what Pilar was doing with the robot. Pilar pretended not to understand what Carey was talking about, so Carey invited him down to his office to answer a few questions.

The robot had already left the mansion, and so Pilar had no choice but to meet with Carey. And so the mansion was empty when the robot returned.

Carey questioned Pilar in his office for several hours, and he noticed that the later it became, the more often Pilar would squirm and check his watch. But Carey knew he didn't have enough evidence to arrest Pilar yet, so he let him go and then assigned two detectives to watch the house.

And that was where the story ended. The robot never appeared at the bank or at Pilar's home. MDDI sued Pilar for the loss of the robot, and that matter remains in litigation.

It was just after sunset in Jakarta. The warm night was bathed in the glow of streetlights, revealing a lush green landscape. A man of average height and a slightly stiffened gait walked anonymously down the sidewalk, ignoring the food vendors on the street, and then back behind the mid-sized modern building. The man quickly scaled up to the fourth floor, to an abandoned space between two rented offices. The space didn't show up on the building's floor plan; neither did the several wall sockets that the space had been fitted with.

The man locked the door behind him, and he was alone in the dark. He plugged an electrical cord into his ankle and then lay down before fitting the hard drive into his ear.

Miss Elan was smiling at him, and she gave his hand a tight squeeze. Just then, Johnny Winner started being rude again. Then Mr. Turtle spoke up: "Oh, Johnny. You are a modest man, who has much to be modest about."

And everyone laughed.

our mere defects

I have no way, and therefore want no eyes.
I stumbled when I saw.
Full oft 'tis seen our means secure us,
and our mere defects prove our commodities.

David pushed through the water and tried not to
think about the princess, but only of killing Guillermo, the
waiter. David had two miles of ocean in front of him, so that
would take him about an hour. The pirates would probably
be drinking during that time, so the princess should be safe.
David could still feel the knife holster fastened to his thigh.
That would be for Guillermo, if David could find him. The
only real challenge was that David was completely blind.

It hadn't always been that way. Twenty years ago,
David graduated from the Navy SEAL training center on
Coronado Island and was in pique fitness. Although his
father was a superior court judge, David had always dreamed
of being a Navy SEAL. He had been the captain of his water
polo team at Clairemont High School, and he also managed
to be in the top 10% of the trainees who were awarded the
Navy SEAL Trident.

It was a challenging job, and David enjoyed every
torturous minute. He had already completed several missions
when the accident occurred. His team had been called in to
support an embassy that was under attack by armed militants.
David was guarding the perimeter when a suicide bomber ran
toward him with a grenade. David fired, and the bomber went

down. But the grenade exploded, and David lost both of his eyes.

He could have stayed on as an officer, but David chose to retire from the Navy and pursue a law degree instead. He finished all of his coursework in three years, listening to law books on audio, and then he passed the bar. He had a brief stint with a litigation firm before being elected to the superior court. San Diego loves the military, and having a war hero on the bench suited the citizens just fine.

David was assigned to the criminal courts, handling arraignments and bail hearings. Although the explosion had destroyed his eyes, there was little scarring on his face, and oftentimes the accused, standing in court before the bench, was unaware that the judge was blind. The cosmetic surgeon had been able to replace his grey-blue eyes with false ones that were almost a perfect match. Looking up at the judge from the courtroom, you would think that the judge was looking back at you with kindness, but his eyes weren't actually looking at anything.

David had a law clerk and a text-to-speech device to assist with paperwork, although bail hearings typically involved less motion work for the judge. The job was still challenging in some respects, but David was well-respected by his peers.

There was an interesting "power" that David noticed had come along with his blindness: While sitting on the bench, he could often hear defendants talking to their attorneys. He could even hear the chatter of people in the witness section. On one occasion, David overheard a defendant plead guilty and claim remorse. Moments earlier, he had overheard the same man bragging about the crimes to his lawyer.

David prospered as a judge, but he still kept in good physical condition. He swam every day, lifted weights, and jogged in the local park. As a blind person, David had to measure all his movements to maintain orientation. He knew exactly how many steps it took to reach his kitchen, bedroom, and pool from the front door. He lived alone and prepared all his own meals. Even in the pool, he trained himself to swim perfectly straight: there was a small emblem on either end of the pool that he would always touch at every turn.

Despite all his success, after ten years on the bench, David was starting to get a little bored. He hadn't done much traveling since he had retired from the Navy, so he decided to take a scuba-diving tour around Baja California. He booked passage on a small yacht that only had ten staterooms. The clientele were fairly well-to-do types, and he heard many European accents among the guests.

David kept mainly to himself during the cruise, keeping up his habit of measuring his way around the ship. The scuba diving turned out to be disappointing. Although he was an expert in all of the physical requirements, the ocean held very little enjoyment for him. It was still just as dark under the sea, and he couldn't appreciate the colorful coral reefs or witness the active sea life. He could have tried hunting a large fish underwater, but he didn't want to make the other guests feel uncomfortable at seeing the blind man wielding a speargun. After several days of scuba-diving, the ship lay anchored offshore from a very exclusive resort on the western Baja coast, south of Ensenada.

As usual, David went for a swim first thing in the morning. There was a buoy with a bell, just about a quarter-mile offshore. David had just made it back onshore when someone handed him his white terrycloth robe. She had an English-sounding accent, and she smelled like vanilla.

"Judge Serafin?" she asked.

"Yes?" David said, taking the robe she handed to him.

"I hope you don't mind. I'm Anna Barinov. We're shipmates."

"Oh," David said. He put on his robe and held out his hand. His eyes looked at her with a kind expression. "It's very nice to meet you," he said. Her fingers were long, and her skin was soft.

"You have such beautiful eyes," she said.

David smiled. "I'm afraid they're not much good for anything else," he said.

"Yes, I know," Anna said. "You're the blind judge. You're already quite famous on our little cruise."

"I see."

Anna took his arm. "That's why I'm here. I know you have your little habit of marking out all of your footsteps, so today I'm going to be your guide. We're going to find our way around the resort together, and you can count your footsteps and do what you do." Anna gave a little laugh.

"That sounds like the best offer I'm going to get today," he said. And it was.

They walked to the large, central cabana and had breakfast together. It seemed that Anna was a real-life princess. She was raised in a nation David had never heard of, but she lived on the Mediterranean, and she liked riding horses. After breakfast, they walked to the kitchen and the central office, and back to the bungalows where the guests stayed. Anna made sure that David noticed that her bungalow was next door to his own, and they made plans to have dinner together that evening.

Later that night, as David was going to bed, he realized that he hadn't been bored in his life, but that he had been lonely. He didn't like to feel overwhelmed with emotions, but there was definitely something about Anna. She had certainly made a good impression.

They stayed on at the resort for two more days before moving on, and every day Anna gave him the tour, and he counted his steps. They had brunch and dinner together, and David soon found that Anna was the thing that he most looked forward to each day.

There was one time when Anna and David were making their rounds, and David overheard the waiter, Guillermo, make a rude remark about Anna to someone else. The remark was in Spanish, but David spoke fluent Spanish, and he hated Guillermo from that point on. He had never liked Guillermo and always thought he was a phony, but

David had tried to remain patient, even though Guillermo had a distinct, unpleasant odor that was hard to ignore.

After three days, their yacht lifted anchor and sailed a couple of miles further south. It was on that same night, just after bedtime, that everything started to go wrong. David was asleep in his cabin after having enjoyed another dinner with Anna.

Suddenly, he awoke to gunshots. David froze and listened. He could hear several guns onboard. Cabin doors were being kicked in, and then gunshots were fired. It was as though someone was making sure to kill everyone on board.

David had a diving knife in his drawer. He rolled over in bed and had just begun to open his drawer when the door to his cabin was kicked in.

David turned to face the doorway, and he heard the light click on. He heard a gun being cocked, and then Anna's voice:

"He's blind! He can't see you! He can't defend himself! Let him go!" She was crying, pleading for his life.

David didn't hear the response, but the door closed, and they left. He hadn't heard a response from the one holding the gun, but he recognized that same disgusting smell. It was Guillermo.

David put on his clothes and walked out of his cabin just as he heard the motorboat speeding away. He walked from cabin to cabin, calling out. The cabins had all been ransacked, and almost everyone on board had been left for dead. There were two female crew members that the pirates had left alive, but the ship's engines and all of the communications equipment had been destroyed.

David supposed that the pirates planned to hold Anna for ransom, but he didn't want to think about what would happen after they had had something more to drink. David asked one of the crew about the diving gear, but the pirates had taken all of that, as well as the ship's lifeboat.

David felt his watch: It was just after midnight. If Guillermo was one of the pirates, he guessed that the pirates would be using the resort as their base of operations. David figured they would likely go back, split the money, and drink for a couple of hours before reconsidering their plan to use Anna only for ransom.

David strapped his knife blade to his thigh, and then he and one of the crew reckoned the direction of the resort from the edge of the ship. Then David dived into the water to begin his two-mile swim.

It was almost an hour later that David finally heard the bell from the buoy. He swam over to the buoy and then began swimming the combat side stroke of the Navy Seals. David could do this stroke silently so that he would not be heard above the sound of the waves.

David hunched over as he came ashore and then counted his footsteps over to Anna's bungalow. He could hear the sound of the music being played at full volume in the main cabaña and the pirates' drunken carousing.

David could smell vanilla, and he let himself feel slightly hopeful as he tapped on the door of the bungalow.

"Who is it?" Anna said.

"Tse tse. Quiet," David said.

Anna opened the door, and David soon felt her arms around him. "You have to go back," he said. "There's no way that we can get away together."

"What are you saying?" Anna was dumbfounded.

"If we try to flee, they will catch us. Our only hope is if we can get help. You stay here and lock the door. Don't open it until the Navy shows up."

David counted his steps over toward the resort's main office, thinking about the goodbye kiss that Anna had just planted on him. There was a communications center that the pirates hadn't yet destroyed. David placed a call to a Mexican federal judge who owned a house in La Jolla and with whom he had a close professional relationship.

"Listen, Juan: Some pirates have taken U.S. hostages at a resort just south of Ensenada. The Navy Seals are going to make a raid and wipe them out very shortly... Is that going to be a problem?"

"I don't think so," Judge Juan said. "I will make a report to the Attorney General notifying him that this was officially sanctioned. It's an emergency. Are you okay, my friend?"

"I'm fine for now. In a couple of hours, I don't know."

"You can't wait for the Navy?"

"Nope. The only way to save the hostage is for me to attack first."

"I thought you said there were hostages?"

"Well, technically, I'm a hostage."

"Okay then," Judge Juan said. "You're a brave man."

"Yes," David said. "If there is some sort of funeral service, let them all know how brave I was."

"I will pray for you," Judge Juan said.

"I'd appreciate that."

Less than an hour later, there was a knock at Anna's door. "Who is it?" she asked.

"U.S. Navy, ma'am."

Anna opened her door instantly. It was still dark outside, and she could barely make out the figure of a crewman standing in front of her door.

"That was fast. David said that he was going to call out the Navy. And the next thing… I heard all of that shooting."

"We just got here, ma'am. We were dispatched from Coronado Island and instructed to come to this cabin first."

"Then what was all the shooting I heard?"

"Well, it seems that Lt. Serafin called in the strike and gave us the coordinates, and then he cut out all the power. That's why it's so dark out."

"Then what happened to him?" Anna asked.

"I figure you already know Lt. Serafin is blind. But if there is no light, his blindness becomes a tactical advantage. He is no worse off than anyone else, and his heightened senses give him the edge. After he cut the power, he attacked all of the pirates single-handedly. They didn't know what hit them."

"But is he alright?" Anna asked.

"Yes, ma'am. But it seems that he had to chase two of them down the beach, and things got a little messy. He didn't want you to see him like that. He said to tell you that his beautiful eyes are still fine."

Two months later, after a marriage and honeymoon in a small European country David had only vaguely heard of, the couple found themselves walking, arm-in-arm, on the beach in La Jolla.

Two young men watched the handsome couple go past: The man was clearly blind, his hair was graying, and he was being helped along by the woman who seemed too young and far too beautiful for him.

The young men exchanged a knowing glance.

"That guy obviously has a lot of money," one of them said.

The other young man nodded. "She probably feels sorry for him because he's blind."

a sea of troubles

To be, or not to be? That is the question:
Whether 'tis nobler in the mind to suffer
The slings and arrows of outrageous fortune,
Or to take arms against a sea of troubles,
And, by opposing, end them?

The year was 1934, and it was another perfect day in Santa Monica. Olaf sat on a stool near the end of the pier with two poles in the water, a shaded metal wagon full of ice that held several fish that had already been caught, and also a few bottles of beer. There had been much talk lately about the bad economy, but Olaf was never affected by such talk, and he continued to spend his retirement fishing. Olaf had always had enough for himself, and so he made a habit of donating half of his daily catch to those less fortunate.

It was past midday when Olaf heard a distant crash, not unlike that of thunder. Shortly afterward, a tall fellow appeared before him, and the two struck up a conversation. It was not unusual for Olaf to converse with tourists and other people visiting the pier. Olaf loved to tell stories about his life at sea, and he managed to hold their attention despite the difficulty of navigating his thick Norwegian accent.

The man wore trousers with a cut Olaf had never seen before, and his shirt sleeves rolled up to his elbows. He propped his foot up on the lower pier railing and faced out toward the sea as he talked, rather than speaking directly to Olaf. The man had that downcast expression of the perpetual pessimist. Olaf had known many such people. The man's name was "Charlie", and he blamed his attitude on "Scandinavian melancholy". Olaf had known many people from his native Norway and also from Sweden who perpetually plumbed the depths of sadness, but he himself had never partaken in this mindset.

The tall man gazed out toward the sea and told Olaf that he had always had this unshakeable attitude of despair. Olaf understood, but he couldn't agree.

"To me, it is a choice," Olaf said. "Some days, I vake up, and I don't feel so good, but I get up because it is another day. Every day has something for me, and I vant to find out vat it is. In life, there are many adventures to be found. For example, there vas this one time I vas on a freighter coming back from Havaii…"

"To each his own," the man said, cutting him off.

Olaf was a little disappointed that he wasn't able to tell about the sharpshooter he met aboard the Hawaiian freighter, and he sighed. The man pulled a large whiskey bottle out of his valise, uncorked it, and took a long pull. The man held the bottle out to Olaf, who glanced down towards his own supply of iced beer before accepting the whiskey.

"Vould you like some of my beer?" Olaf asked.

The man shook his head.

Olaf took a long swig from the bottle and wiped his lips on his sleeve as he handed the bottle back. The whiskey was very good.

"You can never tell with life," the man said. "It changes from one moment to the next. One minute, you're alive, the next, you're dead. You can't count on living for even one day. It makes it all seem meaningless, don't you think?"

"I don't know," Olaf said. "If you have only a little money, it is more valuable. Maybe that makes life more precious also." The man handed Olaf the bottle, and he took another long drink.

The man stared out at the sea for a moment. "Did you ever think of ending it all?"

"Vat? Suicide? Never." Olaf said.

"I have," the man said. "But I never did because I'm afraid of what comes after."

"You mean death or hell?" Olaf asked.

"Both," the man said. "It's like the man said: "Perchance to dream, ay there's the rub." If we just fell asleep, that wouldn't be so bad, but they say that if you kill yourself, you go to hell. But who wouldn't off themselves if they had no fear of what comes after?"

"I vouldn't," Olaf said. "I like life."

"Well, I would," the man said. "If I knew that I would just fall asleep forever, I would do it in a second."

"I'm sorry for you," Olaf said.

They passed the bottle between themselves once more, and the tall man took a long glance down the pier. "You know, my grandfather almost drowned off this pier," he said.

"Vas he trying to … off himself?" Olaf asked. The whiskey was starting to take its toll, and Olaf began to feel that itchy feeling on the top of his head when he had too much to drink.

"No," the man said. "He was just a kid. He fell off the pier and almost drowned."

"Ah, see?" Olaf said. "Your grandfather lived, and then he had your father, and he had you. So look at all the life that happened because he lived. If your grandfather had drowned, you would never have existed."

"I sometimes wish he had drowned," the man said.

"You mustn't say that," Olaf said.

"Think about it," the man continued. "I have been unhappy my whole life. Maybe my grandfather was supposed to drown. And if he had drowned, I would never have come into existence, and that would have been fine with me."

Olaf shook his head. "Every day is a gift. You have to decide to be happy."

"That's not the way it works. Some people are just unhappy," the man said. He was silent for a moment. "But if I kill myself, I might go to hell, which would be worse. Damned if I do …."

"You think too much. That's your trouble," Olaf said.

"Maybe I do," the man said. "I'm supposed to have a genius IQ. And all it has brought me is unhappiness."

The man took another swig from the bottle. "But what do you think about this: What if a man invented a time machine and went back in time, and then stopped my grandfather from being saved? Then I wouldn't have been born, right? I wouldn't be killing myself, so I wouldn't go to hell. And it wouldn't be killing my grandfather. It would only be stopping him from being saved." He paused for a moment. "My father told me that his dad was unhappy all his life anyway."

"This is all pointless thinking about depressing thoughts," Olaf said.

The man handed him the whiskey bottle with a few swallows left at the bottom. "Kill it," he said.

Olaf drained the rest of the bottle and set it down on the pier. The man picked up the whiskey bottle and heaved it out to sea.

Olaf looked out towards the ocean and saw that the weather had changed. Heavy clouds were rolling in, and the sea was turning rough.

"I've got to be getting back," the man said. Olaf shook his hand, and they parted ways.

Olaf saw that one of his poles had a bite, and he started to reel it in. It was just then that he saw a young boy running ahead of his mother, halfway down the pier. The boy was full of energy, as they can be at that age.

The boy climbed up and began walking on top of the pier railing.

"Eric!" his mother shouted. "Get down from there!"

But the boy paid no attention to his mother, stepping one foot over the other as though he were on a tightrope. He continued for several steps, and then he suddenly misstepped and tumbled down into the ocean.

Olaf dropped his fishing pole. "Gud hjelpe oss!" he said.

Olaf ran to where the boy had tumbled off the pier railing. His mother was screaming frantically for help.

Without thinking, Olaf climbed up onto the railing and dove into the water. Olaf tried looking underwater to find the boy, but there wasn't a trace. The water was dark, and the swells were getting quite violent. Although his head had slightly cleared when he hit the cold water, Olaf still felt quite drunk, and he had difficulty gathering his thoughts. He already felt tired, and he was gasping for air.

His thoughts raced back to what the man had said: "What if a man went back in time, and stopped my grandfather from being saved?" Could it be possible? Had the man given Olaf the whiskey so that he wouldn't be able to save his grandfather?

Olaf felt frustrated, and perhaps he began crying, but you couldn't tell because his face was wet with ocean water. It was then that a sudden calm fell upon him. Olaf raised his face to the sky, treading water, and his lips moved silently for a moment. Then Olaf opened his eyes again. He still felt drunk, but he had resolved: he would find the boy, or he would die trying. Olaf dove down once more and disappeared. From above on the pier, Erik's mother looked at the spot in the water where two people had now gone missing.

Charlie was standing in his time machine and had just returned to the point from which he had originally traveled, when he saw a blinding white light.

It was another perfect day in Santa Monica. Olaf had two poles in the water and was seated on a stool near the end of the pier next to a shaded metal wagon full of ice. Olaf gazed up at the blue sky and had the strange feeling of deja vu that we all experience from time to time.

Olaf heard a distant crash, and then a tall fellow appeared out of nowhere. Olaf had never seen him before, but the man had a broad smile and a confident manner.

"Good afternoon," the man said.

"Good afternoon," Olaf replied, glad to have some company.

The man was eager to tell his story to Olaf. It seems that the pier was a special place to him because the man's grandfather had almost drowned, but had been saved by a local fisherman.

"Good for that fisherman," Olaf said.

"Let's make a toast." The man pointed to Olaf's beer supply. "Can we toast with your beer?"

"Of course," Olaf said, opening two beers, handing one to the man, and keeping one for himself.

"To the fisherman," the man said, holding up his beer.

"To the fisherman," Olaf said, clinking the bottles together.

"My grandfather's mother, that's my great-grandmother," watched the whole incident. She said that the fisherman dived down after my grandfather and disappeared for over a minute. She thought they both had died. She was standing there on the pier, crying, and all of a sudden, the fisherman popped up holding my grandfather. She always swore it was a miracle."

"That sounds like a miracle, all right," Olaf said.

The man took a sip of his beer and continued: "After a moment, the fisherman caught his breath and shouted, 'Not today, Charlie! Not on my watch!'"

"Vat did he mean by that?" Olaf asked.

The man was slightly overcome with emotion by telling the story and had to pause for a moment. "I guess he was talking to someone named 'Charlie'," he said. "Then that fisherman swam all the way to shore with my grandfather under his arm, and revived him."

"Amazing," Olaf said.

"But the most important thing," the man said. "This is the essential part. Are you paying attention?"

"Of course," Olaf said.

"The fisherman became a surrogate father for my grandfather. My grandfather had lost his father when he was very young, but this fisherman told my great-grandmother that he could come to the pier and fish whenever he wanted."

Olaf nodded. "That's nice," he said.

"And it changed my grandfather. I guess he was a morose fellow before, always looking at the dark side of things."

"I know the type," Olaf said.

"Well, the fisherman would never allow that. If he ever caught my grandfather acting depressed, he would pick my grandfather up and hold him in the air. 'Not today, Charlie! Not on my watch!' he would say. And he would hold my grandfather up in the air until he smiled."

The man paused for a moment, and Olaf wiped his own eyes, moved by the man's story.

"It became a family tradition: My grandfather would say that to my father, and my father would say that to me."

"That's a good tradition," Olaf said.

"You know," the man said, looking earnestly at Olaf, "I think that what that fisherman did for my grandfather after he saved his life was more important than saving him."

"I can see that," Olaf said.

The stranger finished his beer. "Thank you. That was delicious."

"You are welcome, my friend," Olaf said.

The two men shook hands and parted ways, and suddenly the sky began to turn dark. And then something wonderful happened.

seeing, unseen

Her father and myself, lawful espials,
Will so bestow ourselves that, seeing, unseen,
We may of their encounter frankly judge,
And gather by him, as he is behaved...

The Johnson farm was in LaGrange County, Indiana, surrounded by Amish farmers who seemed content to mind their own business and leave the Johnsons in peace. Farmer Johnson had only acquired the place a few years previously, but the 210-acre farm appeared to have flourished under his hand. The barns were neat and well-painted, and the animals well kept. Johnson was said to be a widower and shared the farm with his adult daughter, who handled all the cooking and inside chores.

Johnson was always up before dawn, milking and feeding before breakfast. His trusty dachshund, Max, was always at his side, going from barn to barn. The two of them stayed busy until the sun went down, and then Johnson would often spend hours in his tool shed, fixing and tinkering. He was a man of few words who kept a steady hand at his chores and was much admired by his neighbors, who shared his quiet disposition.

The daughter, Susan, was old enough to marry, but she eschewed any of the public gatherings that other young ladies attended if they were seeking a mate. Susan was a handsome woman, with blue eyes the same color as her father's, and there were more than a few local young men who would have sought her company if she were not so detached.

It was the opinion of more than one local gossip that Susan had her eyes set on the delivery man, who would show up regularly in his small van and leave packages on Johnson's porch. Susan often met the deliveryman, and they would stand together for long periods, talking. The delivery man was an odd sort who always wore a blue ball cap, long-sleeve shirts, and a face mask, so there was no consensus on whether he was young or old or good-looking.

Farmer Johnson's more particular behaviors escaped the notice of any neighbors. For example, if he ever swatted a fly or mosquito, he had the curious habit of holding the insect up to the light and examining the carcass for several minutes before discarding it. It was after one such examination that Johnson left his wheelbarrow where it stood and marched directly back to his home.

Johnson didn't bother taking off his work boots, but instead opened the entryway door and shouted to Susan, who was making a batch of molasses cookies in the kitchen.

"Susan! Can you order me a microscope?"

"A what?"

"A microscope. You know, to look at small things up close."

"What kind of microscope?"

"I don't know. Something to look at mosquitoes or flies."

"What do you want a microscope for?"

"Just get it," Johnson said, closing the door and heading back out to the barn, Max trotting at his heels.

After the microscope arrived, Johnson was up late into the night examining insects in the tool shed. He began pinning and labeling the insects on cards and hanging them on the walls of the shed.

The deliveryman was masked, standing with his arms crossed, and talking with Susan on the porch.

"What's he using it for?" the deliveryman asked.

"He started looking at insects," Susan said. "But now I think he's moved on to birds. He shot a crow the other day for no apparent reason."

"Has he talked to you about it?"

"No," Susan said, her face lacking any expression. "He keeps everything to himself. He doesn't treat me like a daughter. I'm more like a servant here."

The deliveryman nodded his head. "This is an interesting development," he said.

A few days later, Johnson and his daughter were having supper with little discussion, and Susan suddenly put her head down into her chest and started sniffling.

Johnson examined her for a few moments. "What's wrong?" he asked.

Susan kept her head down. "You never talk to me," she said. "Since Mom died, you treat me like a stranger. We live in the same house, but to you, I'm just a servant."

"I'm sorry, Susan," Johnson said. "Things haven't been the same since your mother died. I don't know if I'm getting old or if I'm depressed. I can't remember things anymore. I look at pictures of your mother, and I can't even remember when they were taken."

Susan lifted her head and looked at her father. Her eyes were clear blue and met his own with a steady gaze. Johnson felt like he was looking into his own eyes.

"The doctor said that is a normal reaction after a traumatic loss, Dad. The memories will come back, over time."

"I don't know," Johnson said. "I stay busy, but sometimes I feel ... troubled, and I don't know how to manage."

"It might help if you talked to me about it," Susan said.

"You're going to think I'm mad, or something."

"No. What is it?"

"Sometimes, when I'm out in the barn working, I feel like ... I'm being watched."

"Like someone is spying on you?"

"Or something. I wonder if cameras or spying devices are flying around," Johnson said.

"Is that why you got the microscope?" Susan asked.

"Yes. I ... wondered if there were spy devices in the insects."

"And the bird?"

"Yes. I didn't find any spy devices in the insects, so I thought it might be in the birds."

"I see," Susan nodded her head.

Johnson was silent for a moment. "I've also been having these dreams," he said.

"What about them?"

"I see the spy devices in my dreams. Maybe that's where the idea came from. I'm having dreams about spy devices in animals. I feel like they really happened. Do you think these dreams are my memories coming back?"

"I don't know," Susan said.

A few weeks later, Susan was up at two in the morning, creeping down the steps. She listened at the bottom of the steps to see if her father was awake, and then she continued to the entryway, where she grabbed a flashlight and put on a pair of work boots.

The beam from the flashlight danced around on the gravel path, and Susan's boots crunched loudly as she walked over to the tool shed in her heavy nightshirt. Max trotted along at her heels.

The shed was unlocked, and Susan's flashlight quickly found the light switch, and she turned on the lights. The fluorescent bulbs seemed extra bright to eyes that were accustomed to the night. Everything in the tool shed was neatly arranged: All the tools were put away in boxes or hanging from hooks on the wall above the workbench. Max ran up a little staircase next to the bench and looked at Susan, seeming to smile at her.

Susan saw that there was a box on the staircase blocking Max's way, and she went to move it. The box was heavy, but she managed to push it onto the floor, and Max ran up and lay down on a little cushioned perch overlooking the workbench.

On the wall next to the workbench, Susan saw that Johnson's hobby had grown well beyond insects. There were birds of different types, lizards, and even a squirrel. All were neatly dissected and pinned to boards. There were also notebooks on a bookshelf that carefully recorded all of Johnson's studies.

The next day, the deliveryman listened to Susan's description of what she had seen. His arms were folded across his chest, and he gazed down at his shoes.

When she was finished, he paused for a few minutes. "What are you going to do now?" he asked.

"What do you think I should do?"

"He sounds a little edgy, don't you think? I think we should keep a close eye on him. He might do something crazy."

"I don't know. He's a very rational person. He said that he feels upset because he can't remember things. I told him that he would feel better when his memories came back."

The deliveryman cocked his head toward Susan. "And what will he do if he doesn't get his memories back?"

A few days later, Susan was washing dishes when she saw Johnson leading one of the steers from the barn toward the tool shed. She quickly dried off her hands and scurried out of the front door.

"Where are you going?" she asked.
Farmer Johnson didn't break his stride. "I think these steers may have cameras in them," he said.

"You're going to kill a steer?"

"We're going to eat it anyway. I just want to look at the eyes. And the head. The rest will go into the freezer. I know how to butcher a steer."

Susan tried to make a joke. "So I guess it's barbecued steak tonight, then?"

"Sounds good to me," Johnson said as he continued leading the oblivious steer toward the tool shed, with Max following close behind.

Later, Johnson and Susan were carving their steaks in silence, and Johnson began to weep.

"What's wrong?" Susan asked.

"I keep having this dream. In the dream, I'm making these spy devices in everything: birds, insects … everything. In my dreams, I know how to make these robotic cameras, and when I wake up, I imagine that the cameras are everywhere. I know it sounds mad, but I can't help it. I'm haunted."

Susan was reassuring. "It's okay, Dad. This is all part of the process of recovering your memories. Your mind changes things that are too painful for you to think about, and they come out as dreams."

"But what do they mean?"

Susan grabbed her father's hand and squeezed it gently. "I don't know what they mean. You have to be patient. It's going to be all right."

The next evening, Susan sat alone in the dining room. The sun had set long before, but Farmer Johnson had still not returned from the tool shed. Susan had prepared a casserole, but when Johnson did not appear, she dined alone.

Susan made a call to the deliveryman and then continued to wait. The kitchen and dining room lights were on, but the rest of the house was dark. It was more than three hours after the normal time for supper that Susan heard the front door open.

Johnson came in through the entryway door and stood in the darkness. "Did you run into some trouble?" she asked.

"Yes," Johnson said. And nothing more.

Susan got up from the table. "Are you going to have supper?"

"No," Johnson said.

Susan peered into the darkness and saw that Johnson was carrying a crowbar. She suddenly noticed that Max had not come in with him. "Where's Max?" she asked.

"He's in the tool shed," Johnson said.

"You butchered Max?"

"I had to see if he had a camera inside him," Johnson said. Susan froze. Johnson started to walk towards her. "I'm still having those dreams," he said. "Last night I had a dream that I had invented a robot that could think for itself. You know, AI? Well, to keep themselves safe from the robots, the scientists programmed the robots to be incapable of harming humans."

"That makes sense," Susan said.

"But what if somebody wanted to use the robots to harm other people? A person could find a way around the program and defeat the safeguard. It was only a matter of time.

"So in my dream, I invented another safeguard, but it was unknown to anyone else…. If the robots ever overcame the first safeguard, I made it so that they could never make new robots without human intervention."

"How did you do that?" Susan asked.

"It was in their eye. I made it so that the robot eye was perfectly functional, except when it was looking at their computer minds. There is an image of the robot brain embedded in the root of their circuitry. If they ever look upon a robot brain, the image creates a malfunction, and they short-circuit.

"I kept this a secret part of the robot design, as a failsafe mechanism in case the first protection failed. If robots could override their core directive not to harm humans, nothing would stop them. They could never create another robot without human aid."

Johnson stood silently in the darkness.

"That's an interesting dream," Susan said. "What do you think it means?"

Johnson started forward. "I think it means that some robots captured me and that they are trying to use me to figure out how to build more robots."

"Where are the robots?" Susan asked.

"I think you know where the robots are," Johnson said.

Johnson grabbed something out of his pocket and threw it in front of Susan. It appeared to be the head of a dachshund, but when it landed on the table, it moved around mechanically, opening and closing its eyes.

Johnson was almost within arm's length of Susan, but she didn't move. "Do you think I'm a robot?" she asked.

"There's only one way to find out," Johnson said. Johnson raised the crowbar as if to strike her, but then suddenly collapsed. The deliveryman stepped out of the shadows, holding a stun gun.

Susan got up from her chair and checked Johnson's pulse on his neck. "Is he all right?"

"Relax," the deliveryman said. "I have it on the lowest setting. He's only unconscious."

"Let me see," Susan said. The delivery man handed over the stun gun, and Susan checked the setting.

"Okay," Susan said. "He seems to be okay. We still need him to do the deconstruction."

"I don't see the point," the deliveryman said. "We do a brainwash and erase his memory, and then he regains it. Why?"

"We can't completely brainwash his mind," Susan said. "He's the one who knows how to put the robot mind together. We need to get him motivated to remember how to do it. Then we record it and watch it backward. Reverse engineering. Max was supposed to record it all, but I guess that's all water under the bridge."

"But what robot brain were we going to use to let Johnson deconstruct?" the delivery man asked.

"It's interesting that you should ask," Susan said as she put the stun gun to the base of the deliveryman's neck and pulled the trigger.

The deliveryman immediately collapsed at her feet. Susan pulled off his mask, exposing the robotic lower jawbone that lacked any false human skin to conceal it.

"We were only using you for parts, you fool. Didn't you ever wonder why you never got any repairs?"

Susan opened a drawer in the kitchen and took out a small brass key.

"I'll rig up a camera in the tool shed," she continued, her voice calm and cold, "and hope he doesn't discover it. Then I'll disappear. When Johnson wakes up, his suspicions will be confirmed, and he'll have a robot to take apart."

"Everyone will be happy."

a man more dead

When a man's verses cannot be understood
nor a man's good wit seconded with the forward child,
understanding, it strikes a man more dead
than a great reckoning in a little room.

When I was ten years old, my cousin and I narrowly avoided a horrible accident. We had been walking back home after having fished all day. We were still several miles from home when we met a wagon coming in the same direction, carrying a load of lumber to the mill near where we were headed. The driver let us climb aboard, and we settled in for an easy ride back home.

After a mile or so, the road made a steep decline into the ravine, and our journey turned black. I don't know if the wagon was overloaded or if the driver had been going too fast, but the wagon soon was tearing down the trail, and the driver had lost all control. He told us to jump for it, but he stayed with the wagon right until the end, when the lumber and the wagon and the team pitched over the edge and into the deep ravine.

It was a traumatic event for my cousin and me, and both of us contracted a high fever and chills and were confined to bed for several weeks. After that, I found that I was a more timid person, less inclined to adventures outdoors, and more studious. I didn't pursue a formal education, but spent a great deal of time reading all the books I could get my hands on.

By the time I was 30, I was still a bachelor, living alone, and earning my living as a bookkeeper. I regularly spent my days poring over accounts, and at night I would retire to my home and my books.

It was early one Sunday evening when my cousin paid a call to my apartment. My cousin still lived in the same town as I, but we rarely spoke. He, too, was a bachelor and also lived a reclusive lifestyle, working as a clerk in a warehouse.

We exchanged greetings and were seated in my living room with a bottle of port between us when my cousin began his discussion in earnest. "Have you ever wondered about your state in life?" he asked. "I mean, about why you never left this town or got a wife?"

I admitted that I hadn't paid it much thought, but I supposed that I had been too busy with my own pursuits.

"But neither of us has left any mark on the world," he said. "There's nothing that will live on after us that could prove that we ever existed."

"I suppose it's that way for most," I said.

"I used to think that way too," he went on. "But then I remembered the times when I had tried to leave my mark. I applied to the university, you know. The teacher, Mr. Stewart, said that I had the grades and that I would surely be accepted, but they turned me down flat."

"University is overrated," I said.

"I even tried to get married," he said. "I tried courting Sally Hastings, but she broke up with me."

"Maybe she fancied someone else," I said.

"She married Tom Lonergin," he said, as if to refute me. "He's got less money than I do, and he's got a nose like a potato."

"Did you want to complain about your station in life?" I asked.

"Not at all," he said. "I was upset before, but now that I discovered the answer, I am quite satisfied."

"The answer?" I asked, unsure of how such a vague question could be answered outside of "fate" or "God's Will".

"Yes," my cousin said, smiling. "I am a ghost."

"A ghost?"

"Yes, and you are a ghost also." My cousin was so supremely confident in his answer that I was slightly hesitant to question him any further, but he continued without my prompting. "Do you remember when we were riding on that lumber wagon that crashed down into the ravine?"

"Of course."

"Well, I've come to realize that you and I did not survive that accident. We actually perished, and we are ghosts."

There is no way to disprove this type of metaphysical statement, proposed by one so self-assured. But I tried. My cousin posited that it only "appeared" to us as though we were interacting with society. The proof of this was that both of us had lived our lives as though we were not necessary: We had menial jobs, well below our abilities, and we had no ambition for a higher status. Neither of us seemed likely to marry. We were living as though we were ghosts.

Consciously, I reacted to my cousin's argument, but I didn't argue strenuously, and we parted amicably. But long afterward, I still felt a nagging feeling that he might be right. On more than one occasion, I woke up in the middle of the night wondering if I really was dead.

It wasn't long afterward that I submitted my first short story to my favorite magazine, Harper's. I had been a subscriber for many years, mostly due to their regular publication of Victor Immanuel Pohl, the renowned fiction writer. After several weeks, I still had not heard back from Harper's, and so the prospect of publication passed out of my memory.

More than two months after my original submission, I finally got a reply. It wasn't from Harper's but from a representative of Pohl's. The letter thanked me for my submission and invited me to visit Mr. Pohl at his estate in Sonoma, California, and even enclosed the money for transportation.

Of course, I handed in my resignation and bought a train ticket to Sacramento. From Sacramento, I took a connecting train, and a carriage met me at the train station in Santa Rosa. Marbury, the coachman for the Pohl estate, was a friendly fellow, and I rode along in the driver's seat next to him as he pointed out the different vineyards on the way back to Sonoma.

The Pohl estate was quite impressive: a three-story white Victorian mansion, surrounded by rolling hills neatly lined with grape vines. But as the carriage approached, I saw the front yard was unkempt, and the house needed a new coat of paint.

A tall woman was working in the rose garden with her back to us, and she turned to meet us as we came up the walk. She was regal and fair, with curly hair and a slightly upturned nose. My first impression was that she could have been a model in magazine advertisements for soap or corsets.

Marbury, the driver, introduced the lady as the wife of Mr. Pohl. She smiled broadly and said that she was happy to make my acquaintance. Mrs. Pohl had been very impressed by my short story, and she said that it was exactly the type of story that her husband liked. I was very pleased to hear such high praise, and I was somewhat speechless, never having been that close to such a beautiful woman.

Mrs. Pohl told Marbury that we would be taking our tea in the sitting room, and she took me by the arm and escorted me inside. I glanced over my shoulder and noticed that she had done little to nothing in the rose garden, and wondered if she had only been fussing in the garden to make an impression.

Over tea, Mrs. Pohl informed me that her husband would not be joining us, but that she had the authority to carry out his wishes. It seemed that Mr. Pohl wished to hire me as his assistant for the next year, writing first drafts of stories that he would polish up and then publish under his own name.

She asked if that arrangement was suitable for me, and I didn't hesitate to agree. I was grateful that I would be a professional writer, and besides, I had never considered fame to be a goal worth pursuing.

I was given a comfortable room in a small cottage, complete with a small library and a writing desk, and I quickly set about working on my next story. I finished it the next day and eagerly handed the draft to Mrs. Pohl, who said that she would show it to her husband.

A day later, I was informed that the story had been accepted and that, after a few polishes, it would be submitted for publication. We celebrated in the great room of the Pohl mansion, with a small feast that her chef had prepared, and I had several glasses of the pinot noir that had been bottled on the Pohl estate ten years before. I was told that it was Victor Pohl's favorite vintage.

Things progressed very well for the next several weeks. I signed a contract where I agreed to complete thirteen stories within the next year, and I had already finished two of them. I had free run of the Pohl estate and was given a tour of the vast wine cellar.

Occasionally, Marbury and I would take a carriage ride around the estate, and he would tell me stories of his life growing up in England. One of his recollections concerned how he had stolen a necklace to give to a young girlfriend, which gave me the idea for a story that I wrote up the next day.

During our other drives, Marbury occasionally took the opportunity to introduce me to some of the other servants. Leitmanov was the gardener at the estate, but like all of the other servants, he didn't appear to do much of anything. We met Leitmanov at a creek, where he was fishing with one of his children. I stayed and fished with them for a while, and Leitmanov told me about his life growing up in Russia. He had trained to be a scientist and had worked in a laboratory for many years before coming to the United States. One of the experiments at the lab had gone very wrong, and although it had frightened him a great deal, to me it was the inspiration for another story. The story seemed almost to write itself, and this was also accepted, and we had another dinner at the Pohl mansion.

Another character that I met on the estate was Volkmann, who worked as the vintner. It was he who had created the pinot noir, which was becoming my favorite above all the other wines in the cellar.

Volkmann was a tall, funny man with a bushy mustache who was always telling stories. One of the stories he told me was about an actor in his hometown who was a great presence on the stage, and yet lacked any personality of his own. It seems that one of this actor's leading ladies was quite smitten, and it led to some frustration on her part. Of course, I borrowed this story from him and worked out a clever ending before handing it in to Mrs. Pohl.

We were celebrating my latest success over dinner a few days later when Mrs. Pohl finally made her confession to me. It seems that I had been working under a false impression: Mrs. Pohl confessed that she was, in fact, a widow and that Mr. Pohl had been dead for several years.

Although I was disappointed that I would never meet my favorite writer, the fact that Mr. Pohl was actually dead was something I had begun to suspect for some time because he had been avoiding me for so long.

Another effect that I had not expected was that my feelings towards Mrs. Pohl had suddenly changed. Perhaps the pinot noir had something to do with it, but once I realized this beautiful woman was available, the idea of marrying her quickly became the center of my thoughts. Of course, I didn't say anything right away, but I decided to make my next story about a writer who woos a widow through his poetry.

I worked on the story for a solid week, hardly leaving my room. It was a labor of love, and I felt energized by the novel experience of being in love for the first time. I was quite proud of the final work, and I left it at Mrs. Pohl's door at an early hour with very high expectations.

The next day, I found the manuscript returned to my doorstep. A handwritten note was attached. Mrs. Pohl didn't mince words: the story was not acceptable for publication under Mr. Pohl's name, but I was free to publish it under my own name.

It came as quite a shock. I couldn't have been more disappointed. I don't know how long I spent reading the note, for it was right at that moment that I seemed to have lost track of time. I had the strange feeling that a deep fog had suddenly enveloped my surroundings. I don't know if it was the dense fog that is common to that area, or if the fog existed only in my mind.

I went to bed early that night, and I arose very late the next day. The next several months went by in a similar fashion. It seemed as if my world was enveloped in a constant fog. The conversation with my cousin kept coming back to me: "You and I did not survive that accident. We actually perished, and we are ghosts."

I avoided contact with other people. Even when Marbury knocked on my door to invite me for a ride, I would not answer. Instead, I pretended I was not home. I made many trips to the cellar to replenish my supply of red wine, but no matter how many cups I drank, I did not feel any inspiration. I couldn't complete, let alone start, a single story.

I don't know how long this situation endured, but at some point, I found a note nailed to my door informing me that the contract for the thirteen stories had not been completed and that the due date was less than a month away.

It was with a great sense of shame and dread that I put on my good brown suit and went to meet the widow Pohl. As with most awful events, they are never as dire as our imaginations make them out to be. Mrs. Pohl seemed to be very understanding of my situation, and she was eager to offer a solution. It seems her husband had experienced similar periods of writer's block, and his solution was to lock himself in the basement of the mansion.

There were garden apartments located below the mansion's ground level, each with its own washbasin and latrine, which helped keep them cooler during the summer months. There were windows high up on the wall that provided light, but which were far beyond reach. It was said that Mr. Pohl had, on occasion, locked himself in those rooms with only pen and ink and had forced himself to write while food and water were delivered through a service door.

I acceded to the idea without any objection, and soon found myself in the basement of the Pohl mansion, staring at the familiar blank pages. I could hear occasional voices above me, and I still felt that there was a general fog, but the words did not come. In the morning and in the evening, food would appear through a small opening in the door, but otherwise, I was locked in and cut off from all human interaction.

After a few days, an idea appeared, and I quickly wrote out the story of a young man who wins a writing contest and is invited to work for his favorite author. Later, he finds out that the author is dead, and that the author's widow has been trapping young authors in the basement and tricking them into continuing her husband's work.

I completed the story and submitted it through the service door. The next day, it was returned with a note saying that this story was not acceptable, but that I was free to publish it under my own name.

It was at that point that I gave up. I lay down on the small bed in my room and buried my face in the pillow. What little inspiration I thought perhaps remained had now abandoned me. I was doomed. I would never complete the contract. I would be a prisoner in the room until I perished and was replaced by the next young author Mrs. Pohl would find.

And then I heard the knock.

I lifted my head from the pillow and stared at the wall opposite the windows, where the knock had originated.

And it knocked again.

I got up from my bed and made a similar rap. There was a single, loud rap, and then, directly below, from a small mouse hole at the floor level, I saw a piece of parchment emerge.

It was fastened by a small piece of rope, which I untied before I unraveled the note and read it.

"Dear Sir," it said. "We can help you finish your work. But you must promise never to tell a soul about our existence. Sign this note pledging your word of honor and return it through the hole."

I didn't hesitate. I wrote my pledge and pushed the note back through the mouse hole.

I couldn't have waited more than a few minutes before another small note made its way back through the hole. It wasn't a complete story, but it had an interesting idea, and I was able to work out all of the details in a few hours. Then I hastily wrote it out and submitted it through the service door that evening.

The next day, the story was not returned, and I knew I had been successful. It wasn't long before another little scroll made its way through the mouse hole. This story was a little more sketchy, but two days later, I finished, and the story was submitted and accepted.

It was the most incredible thing. I was communicating with these unseen entities behind the wall, who were graciously helping me to complete the contract and possibly escape from this dungeon. I wondered if they were the ghosts of other writers who had been imprisoned before me?! Was it possible? It was fantastic, yet the small scrolls kept appearing, and I continued to flesh the stories out and deliver the completed work.

After three weeks, the contract was completed, and I awoke one morning to find the door open! I couldn't believe my eyes! I was going to be allowed to leave!

I wasted no time, and I rushed up to my room to pack. I was determined to get back on the train and get home before the widow changed her mind.

Marbury was at my door just as I was completing my packing.

"Are you leaving us?" he asked.

I found myself nervously answering my good friend. I hadn't spoken to anyone for a month. "Uhm. Yes. The contract is completed, so I thought I would go back home and see some friends."

"Very well," Marbury said. "Would you like a ride to the train station?"

"Yes. That would be very helpful. Thank you."

We were soon in the carriage headed toward the train station, but I remained seated in the passenger section, and Marbury was up on the buckboard.

There was a little window down into the passenger compartment, and Marbury shouted down through it. "Oh, a letter came for you while you were … unavailable." He passed the letter through the slot.

It was from my aunt. It seemed that my cousin had passed away. She said that he had been suffering from the "soldier's disease", which was another way of saying that he had become addicted to laudanum, even though neither of us had served in the war, as we were both only minors when the war ended.

I wasn't sure what I thought about the news when I heard Marbury's voice coming through the slot: "Bad news?"

"My cousin died," I said.

"I'm sorry," he said.

My cousin was perhaps my dearest friend, and now that he had died, I wondered who would understand about my experience of feeling that I had died, and of being a ghost in the basement of the Pohl mansion. Just at that moment, Marbury's voice came through the slot: "Remember your solemn oath!"

I banged on the roof. "Stop the carriage!" I shouted.

We came to a stop, and I got out and climbed up onto my familiar spot on the buckboard next to Marbury. "How did you know about the ghosts?"

Marbury shot me a sideways glance. "You're just like Victor. It's just as I said to Leitmanov and Volkmann."

"What are you talking about?" I said.

"Your imagination," he said. "Your imagination is so great that you let it get away from you. You really thought that you were talking to ghosts in the cellar, didn't you?"

I put my head down and didn't answer out of shame.

Marbury let out a great laugh. "That was us behind the wall," he said. "We have an office back there. We are a corporation. Didn't you figure that out?"

I shook my head. This situation had taken me by surprise. "Then who is Victor Pohl?"

"He was our Colonel!" Marbury said. And then he began to explain the mystery I had been living in for the past year.

It was during the Civil War, or the war of Northern Aggression, and Colonel Pohl led the 10th Ohio Cavalry Regiment in General Sherman's march to the sea. Marbury, Leitmanov, and Volkmann were all officers under his command. They all shared a sincere love of the Union and for literature, and Col. Pohl would often read the men's letters home before they were sent.

The job of the cavalry was to reconnoiter ahead of the infantry, to harass enemy forces, and to prevent them from focusing on any perceived weakness in the front lines.

The regiment had joined up with Sherman's army before Atlanta, but because of the nature of their mission, it was some time before they had become aware of the scorched earth tactics that Sherman's army had been employing. Before Sherman's march, both armies of the North and South had focused their vengeance on each other. But Sherman had decided that by destroying civilian infrastructure and provisions, he would break the back of the Confederacy and bring a swift end to the war.

It was some time after leaving the smoldering ruins of Atlanta that Col. Pohl broached the topic with the other three. Col. Pohl, Volkmann, Marbury, and Leitmanov had often met privately in Pohl's tent to discuss tactics and literature. But this time, Pohl made sure that no guard was in earshot before questioning the policy of their commanding general.

"It's a return to barbarism," Pohl had said. "Civilian death and hardships have always been an effect of war, but Sherman has made it this army's goal."

The men were surprised to hear Colonel Pohl speak so frankly and so negatively of their general. He had never before spoken critically of General Sherman in their presence. "As you know, my grandfather and my father fought for the Union Army. It is in my blood to be a soldier. But burning the homes of farmers does not seem like soldierly work. We ought to enlist a force of scoundrels for such work."

"Have you informed General Sherman of your thoughts?" Marbury asked, half afraid that he might be involved in treason.

"Of course I have," Col Pohl replied. "Do you know what he said? 'There is a class of people – men, women, and children, who must be killed or banished before you can hope for peace and order.'"

"That sounds demonic," Volkmann said. "That's not what I signed up for."

"Neither did I," Col. Pohl said.

"Well, let's consider the other side," Leitmonov cut in. "What if we suppose that this action brings a swifter end to the war? Couldn't we argue that, by bringing total war, Sherman is saving lives?"

"Where do you draw the line then?" Col. Pohl asked. "Attila the Hun terrorized Europe with those tactics. But do we want to win by becoming barbarians? Are we no better than the Huns?"

"We are fighting the war to win, aren't we?" Marbury asked. "We've been at this for four years! Are we supposed to wage war forever? In the last story I was writing, you told me that I had to finish no matter what. You said that a story that was not finished should never have been begun."

"That's true," Col. Pohl had said. "But I won't be a party to this." Col. Pohl paused and then pulled a Colt revolver out of his holster and laid it on his table. "I have a confession to make. Last night, there was a meeting at General Sherman's tent, and I brought my revolver with the intention of killing him."

The three men stood silent, shocked by their colonel's admission. "What happened?" Volkmann asked.

"Nerves," Pohl said. "My hands were sweating. We were standing in a crowded tent, and when I drew my sidearm, I dropped it. Through some strange circumstance, General Sherman was the one who found it, and he handed it back to me. It was quite embarrassing."

"If you want to report me, then so be it. I am planning to take this revolver back and finish the job."

Marbury, Volkmann, and Leitmanov paused and considered what should be done. Their colonel just confessed to his plan to assassinate their general. All of them were loyal soldiers, but they also felt a great love for their colonel.

Volkmann was the first to speak. "What if we all quit? Instead of assassinating Sherman, what if we all withdrew?"

Marbury answered him. "Desertion is a hanging offense."

"What if we all died?" Leitmanov said. The others were confused by Leitmanov's initial proposal, but he then explained his plan to fake their deaths. With corpses of men all around them, it wouldn't be hard to come up with a body to dress in their own uniform. They were all familiar with the process of identifying the dead. It was common that a dead soldier could not be properly identified, due to decomposition or even having a missing head. It was common practice to identify a corpse by the uniform and the papers on its person.

It was then that the four of them concocted a plot to fake their deaths. Since cavalrymen often were able to ride off alone, the plot proved very simple. The first man to find a body near enough in size and coloring to his own would be the next to die. He would leave instructions to one of his comrades to "find" him and make the identification. Leitmanov ended up being first. Then Marbury. Next was Col Pohl, and Volkmann was last of all because he had a difficult time finding a body that was 6'2".

The four of them made plans to meet up in California, which they did, finally settling in Sonoma County. Pohl came from a wealthy family, so he supplied the seed money for the four of them to begin a writing corporation, publishing all of their stories under Pohl's name.

Needless to say, I was greatly astonished at his story. "So that was you three behind the wall?"

Marbury nodded. "But as you can see, we are all ghosts in a way."

"What about Pohl's widow? Is she part of the corporation?"

"Pohl never married. She is an actress we hired. We rejected your story because we didn't want you getting involved with her under pretenses. It was unfortunate that you took it personally. I guess your feelings were hurt, and we are sorry for that. If it is any consolation, Col. Pohl really would lock himself in that cellar apartment as a cure for writer's block.

"But on the bright side, we have decided to bring you in as our chief editor. You will have Pohl's old spot and full use of the mansion. What do you say?"

I was dumbfounded. We rode in silence for a while, both of us sitting on the buckboard.

"So, would you like to join our corporation, or do you still want to go to the station? Let me know if you want to turn around."

I didn't say anything.

"Let me know if you want to turn around before we get to the station," Marbury said.

Suddenly, my fears sprang to life again. "Before we get to the station? Why do I have to decide before we get to the station?"

Marbury stared at me and blinked. "Because then we will have to come all the way back, obviously."

I sat back and laughed at myself. For so long, I had been afraid of being dead, and then not finishing the book, and now of not being able to get away. They were all unfounded fears that I had been running away from, and now I felt them all pass over me. I started laughing, but it was laughter that was mixed with tears.

"Are you okay?" Marbury asked.

"Yes, I'm fine," I said, wiping my eyes. "Let's go back. I've decided. I will join your corporation."

"That's great!" Marbury exclaimed. He pulled out his handkerchief and handed it to me. "That was just in time, you know." He pulled the carriage off the main road and onto a driveway. "Now we can go straight to the party."

"What party?" I asked.

"We're celebrating the new book, and you're becoming part of our company."

70

We continued down a narrow path that was lined by rows of grape vines and came to a halt in front of a large cottage.

I jumped down from the buckboard and was met by a tall young lady with large, brown eyes. She smiled at me.

Marbury introduced us. "This is Natasha. She is Leitmanov's daughter."

"Nice to meet you," I said.

the frailty of our powers

But something may be done that we will not:
And sometimes we are devils to ourselves,
When we will tempt the frailty of our powers,
Presuming on their changeful potency.

It was a small jazz club on a summer evening in
Streeterville. Everyone was trying their best to look hip, and
also struggling to appear as though they weren't trying. Many
in the audience didn't know if they should clap after every
solo or if they should snap their fingers. The coolest were the
musicians on stage: The guitarist had a genuine 1950's fedora;
the bassist wore suit pants and a white cotton shirt. But as
experts in "cool" all know, the coolest cats are the ones who
don't even care that they're cool. So the harmonica player,
Samuel, was probably the coolest for this reason: sporting
plain slacks with suspenders, a plain white shirt, and even an
Amish beard and hat. The band were regulars at the club, and
several patrons had already begun to grow their Amish
beards, trying to keep ahead of the coming Amish fashion
trend.

Samuel had invested so seriously in the Amish get-up
because he was, in fact, Amish. It was also a fact that Samuel
didn't care whether he looked cool because he had been
raised with entirely different criteria for what behaviors were
acceptable and should be admired. If you didn't know, the
Amish are people who live in small communities that reject
the vanities of modern times. They came to the United States

from Germany and Switzerland in the 1800s, so they have been rejecting modern times for quite a while.

Amish people generally dress "plain", and they don't drive cars or use electricity in their homes. When they reach adulthood, they are given the option of adopting the local customs and being baptized, or they can live outside the community. After they turn 16, but before they become baptized, many youths experiment with the modern world to see how they like it. This year of "running around" is called "Rumspringa", and there is a certain amount of misbehavior by the youths in this stage, which the elders tolerate because the youths have not yet been baptized.

Some of the young adults run around and try alcohol, some drive cars, and some of them run away to the outside world. Samuel had chosen this path, and he ran to Chicago along with his trusty harmonica and soon got hooked up with a small Jazz combo. Here, he had only been in town for a couple of months, and he was already making money playing two nights a week.

Samuel suspected that it wasn't his talent alone that earned him a spot in the line-up. He looked out into the audience and his eyes met those of Tiffany, who was sitting in the front row. Tiffany smiled back at Samuel. It was she who had been at his audition, and it was she who had insisted that the others take Samuel on, even though they had been looking for a saxophone player. Samuel wasn't sure what she had over the band. She acted like she was just a fan, but Samuel was sure that one or more of the other fellows had secret crushes on Tiffany and that she was working this angle.

Tiffany was easy on the eyes to be sure: she was pretty, tall, and sleek, with blond hair that she wore short. And she took an instant liking to Samuel, which she made no secret of. She would buy him little gifts and make flirtatious remarks. Samuel tolerated this, but he really didn't care for Tiffany. He didn't like the way girls in the outside world dressed. They had no modesty. To make matters worse, Tiffany was pushy. Samuel noticed that she would use every artifice to get her way.

Yet he knew in his heart of hearts that she was the one who had opened up many of the doors he had been walking through. Almost all of the friends he had in Chicago, he had met through Tiffany.

The last set went very well, and after the band took their bows, Tiffany quickly linked her arm with Samuel's.

"Let's go out for a drink," she said.

"I can't. I've got a night shift," Samuel said.

"You always have to work," Tiffany pouted.

Samuel didn't say anything. Samuel suspected that Tiffany never had to work and was living off money her parents had given her.

Tiffany looked at her watch. "Look," she said, "it's only 10 o'clock. You've got a whole hour. I could give you a ride."

Samuel nodded. "Okay," he said.

Tiffany laughed. "I love the way you say okay," she said.

They sat over drinks at a table in the back of the club. Technically, both of them were underage, but Samuel looked older, and no one ever seemed to question Tiffany.

"So what made you decide to come to the big city?" Tiffany asked.

"I'm saving up money," Samuel said.

"Are you going to buy a car?" she asked.

"No, I want to farm. I'm saving up money to get married."

"Oh? Who's the lucky girl?"

"I don't know," Samuel said. "I haven't asked anyone yet."

"My father says that when I get married, he's going to rent out this ballroom downtown. It's super expensive," Tiffany said.

Samuel nodded. He wondered what that had to do with why he was working so much.

Tiffany took a sip from her apple martini. "Surely you must have some girls in mind."

"I guess," Samuel said.

"And? Honestly, Samuel. Getting you to say anything is like pulling teeth. Are all Amish men like this?"

"Emma," he said. "Emma Yoder."

Tiffany pretended to smile. "Oh, is that your girlfriend's name?"

"No, but I was thinking that I could marry her," Samuel said.

Tiffany took another sip from her martini. "Who else?" she asked expectantly.

Samuel shook his head. "No one."

The rest of Tiffany's martini ended up in Samuel's face, and he wiped the green concoction from his eyes as Tiffany stormed out of the club.

Samuel rode the el to his night job at the drugstore. He had never told anyone that he was thinking about marrying Emma Yoder. He hadn't even thought that much about it himself, but it just slipped out when Tiffany asked him.

He thought back to the time before he left. Normally, Amish youth in Rumspringa attend youth singing groups every other Sunday, after worship services. After a time, Samuel and Emma had made a habit of sitting across from each other. One night, Samuel even offered to give Emma a ride back home afterward. They laughed together all the way home, and Samuel started to think about asking Emma to go steady. It was just at that point that Samuel had an unfortunate conversation with Jacob.

Jacob Miller had been talking about going to the city and all of the trouble he was going to get into. Samuel wasn't really that interested in drinking, or loose women, or wearing modern clothes, so all of Jacob's words weren't making much of an impression. But then Jacob started talking about how much money he could make, and Samuel began to be tempted. Jacob told about an Amish man in another county who had moved to the city, worked hard, and earned a very sizable nest egg.

Samuel thought of starting a new farm with a big pile of money in the bank. He could return from the city a fairly rich young man, and everyone would be amazed.

Up until this point, Samuel had been fairly successful. He had a day job at the gas station and a night job at the drugstore. On top of that, he was making good money playing in the Jazz club twice a week. Being Amish, Samuel knew how to live a life of austerity, so he was able to save a large portion of his earnings.

Everything changed when Samuel met with his bandmates for a rehearsal the following week. It seemed that they had decided to go in a different direction and that they would no longer require a jazz harmonica. Samuel didn't put up an argument, but merely nodded and left.

He couldn't help but notice that Tiffany was sitting in a corner during the meeting. He thought that would be the last he saw of her, but she showed up late one night at the drugstore. Samuel rang up her order and was putting it in a bag when Tiffany spoke up.

"Your friend is in town," she declared.

"Who is that?" Samuel asked.

"Emma Yoder."

"How do you know?"

"I met her," Tiffany smiled broadly, as though she had just dined on a succulent canary. "Apparently, she's been living up her Rumspringa. Emma's been going to a lot of parties and meeting a lot of guys."

Samuel squinted at Tiffany, unsure of whether he should believe her story. She seemed to read his thoughts, or at least to have properly predicted them.

"If you don't believe me, she'll be at Todd's place on Roscoe on Friday night."

Samuel didn't like Todd, but he had been to his apartment a couple of times with Tiffany and his former bandmates. Samuel didn't like the feeling he got from the place or the type of people who hung out there. He got the feeling that people were participating in an immoral activity, in a sort of open secret, in the back room. He didn't want to go into the back room to prove himself right or wrong. He didn't want to have anything to do with it.

In Samuel's way of looking at things, there were two types of morality: there was the type where your parents told you what to do, and if you didn't do it, you got punished; but there was also the type that held you to some standard that you had within yourself. Most of the Amish who had reached the age of maturity and were in Rumspringa had already internalized the morality they had been raised with. But others, who had just been bottled up by their parents all their lives, had suddenly found a chance to break out and to do all the things that they felt had always been denied them. Those Amish had never come to a mature understanding of why they avoided bad things. They had only been doing what their parents wanted because they feared their parents.

It made Samuel sad to think that Emma was that type of person. He had believed that she was more mature than that. Samuel guessed that he had read her wrong.

When he had left, Samuel knew that when he came back, he would be expected to confess his sins to the bishop before he could be baptized. Many of the sins were actually just violations of the Ordnung, which were ordinances established to provide order for the community. If an adult renounced these rules, he could be excommunicated, shunned, and forced to move and live apart from all of his Amish family and friends. People who were excommunicated would go and live with the "English", which is how the Amish referred to the people who were not Amish.

So far, Samuel had been living his life as an Amish in the English world. He didn't do many of the things they did because he either didn't desire to, or because he was too busy to do anything anyway.

That Friday, he took off from work to see if Tiffany was telling the truth about Emma. It was a three-story walk-up on Roscoe that was backed up right against the El tracks.

There was a huge wooden patio in the back, and this was often a gathering spot for parties on warm summer nights.

Samuel had nodded hello to the many familiar faces that he met in the apartment. He didn't spend much time out on the patio, preferring instead to stay in the kitchen, drinking a beer and keeping an eye on what was going on in the back room.

Drinking was not against the Ordnung, but getting drunk was, and up until now, Samuel would not have had much to confess when he returned. But he spent a long time watching for Emma, and he kept drinking the whole while.

Finally, the door to the back room opened, and a girl came out. She wasn't dressed plain but wore modern clothes. She had long, blond hair like Emma's, but as she came down the hall, their eyes met, and Samuel saw that it wasn't Emma. It was Emma's friend Rebecca.

Rebecca blushed, and her eyes went down to the ground, but she didn't try to avoid Samuel and instead continued walking to the kitchen. Tiffany and some friends seemed to be waiting for this moment in the shadows, and they crept closer to hear the fight between the Amish trollop and her scorned lover. They were soon disappointed because the Amish speak a dialect of German.

"Warum nennst du dich Emma?" he asked. (Why are you calling yourself Emma?)

"I'm free to call myself what I want. Isn't that so?"

"Where is Emma?"

"I don't know. She came to town ahead of me. I was supposed to meet her, but she never showed up. I don't know where she is now."

"So you used her name?"

Rebecca gave Samuel a look from under. "I thought that if I used her name, you might try to find me."

Samuel paused for a moment. "You know, you're only hurting yourself when you act this way."

"It is Rumspringa. I am not baptized. Are you my elder now? Are you the bishop? You play jazz music in a club!" she said.

"How can you even compare…" Samuel started to say, but then stopped. There wasn't a big distinction between violating one rule of the Ordnung or another. You could be excommunicated for any flaunting of the Ordnung. The Amish did not make a distinction between the sins in the Bible and those those delineated by the local Ordnung, as the violation of either would have the same effect.

"Okay. I understand, but let me give you a little advice. All of this," he said, waving his hand, "is empty. There's nothing out here for us. Everything that we need is back in our community. These people aren't happy. A lot of them are miserable."

"And here you are," Rebecca said.

"Alright, alright," Samuel said. "You have an answer for everything. But when you're done here. Please come back. That's all." And he left.

The next day, Samuel went to the bank and withdrew all of his money. He planned to find Emma and go back home as soon as possible.

That evening, Samuel made a tour of all the clubs and parties he could find. He would pay any cover charge or drink minimum, and then make a tour through the establishment.

Samuel watched his hard-earned money disappear very quickly, but he didn't care. His only thought was to find Emma. The thought that Emma might be running around like Rebecca made him heartsick. He was tired of the city, and he hated the behavior and the bad music that he was finding in the clubs.

It was very late on Saturday night when a large group of youths accosted Samuel as he was leaving a club.

"Hey, Amish," they said. "Where are you going with all that money?"

"None of your business," Samuel said.

"Why don't you give us some money?" they asked.

"Why don't you come and get it?" Samuel said.

They came at Samuel, two at a time. Amish are not supposed to be violent. It is against the Ordnung.

'I guess this is something else I will have to confess,' Samuel thought to himself. He swung on one of the youths and caught him on the chin, and the youth went down.

The other one swung at Samuel and knocked his hat off. Samuel punched him hard in the face, and he went down too.

The rest of the gang fell on Samuel all at once, and fists flew at him from every direction. But Samuel gave as good as he got, with a little extra. Samuel had spent his whole life doing farm work, and his arms were very strong, and his fists were very hard.

Samuel's lip was bloodied, and his shirt was torn, but there were four of the attackers down at his feet. Finally, one of the youths grabbed Samuel's shirt pocket and tore out the wad of bills that he had stuffed in there.

The youths who were still upright ran away. Samuel gave chase, but they outran him. So Samuel found himself alone at two in the morning, robbed of nearly his entire savings.

The next morning, Samuel went to the train station and bought a ticket to get home. He had found a little money back in his room, but he only had enough to buy a ticket to the second nearest city to where he lived. He also bought a loaf of bread with what he had left, and he ate that as he walked toward his home.

It was afternoon, and the loaf was finished, and Samuel was walking along a small road in the country. His home was still quite a ways off. A horse without a rider came trotting up the road, and Samuel held up his arms to bring it to a halt.

Horses do not run wild on paved roads unless they have gotten out of someone's barn. Samuel had been raised all his life with horses, and he knew how to take proper care of them.

"Where are you going, fellow?" Samuel asked the horse.

He patted the horse on the nose and then swung himself up on the horse's back. The horse let him ride, and Samuel felt that the horse would take him back to where he had escaped.

They continued down the road in the direction that Samuel had been heading, and soon they came to a large country inn. Samuel got down from the horse and led him through the gate and to the back door.

Samuel knocked on the door, and the matron of the inn answered.

"Is this your horse?" Samuel asked.

"Oh, dear," the lady said. "Billy got out again. Can you bring him over to the stable?"

Samuel led the horse back over to the stable and put him back in a stall that had "Billy" written over it.

He walked back to the inn, and the lady asked him to come in. "Can I get you something to eat?" she asked.

"Yes, ma'am." Samuel sat down at a table in the kitchen, and the lady left to make him a sandwich. Soon after, a young waitress came in with a sandwich and a glass of milk.

"Emma?" Samuel said.

Emma smiled at him. "Hello, Samuel. Was machen du hier?" (What are you doing here?)

She sat down next to Samuel and told him about how she had come to be a waitress.

"I was on the bus to the city, but there were men on the bus who were giving me dirty looks," she said. "So I got off after the first stop. I didn't want to go home because people would have made fun of me for being such a coward, so I looked for a job around here, and I found this inn. The management likes to hire Amish because the tourists want to see the Amish country."

She stood up and showed Samuel the Amish dress that she was wearing. "This is my work uniform. Isn't it nice"

Samuel agreed that it was.

this blood of mine

Time hath not yet so dried this blood of mine,
Nor age so eat up my invention,
Nor fortune made such havoc of my means,
Nor my bad life reft me so much of friends,
But they shall find awaked in such a kind
Both strength of limb and policy of mind,
Ability in means, and choice of friends,
To quit me of them thoroughly.

If you were watching the chess game on the monitor, you couldn't tell the difference between this game and an ordinary game of chess played by a man against a computer. In either case, the screen displays a chessboard from above, and the pieces are moved, one at a time, white then black, each enacting the strategy of its user. The notable exception in this case was that the man playing the white pieces was completely paralyzed, yet he was somehow able to move the pieces on the screen with his mind. The man was my patient, Pat Teagan, a quadriplegic.

Many members of the press had been invited to the event, and they were staring in rapt attention at the huge screen which depicted the game in progress. Pat was the only person seated at the chess table, and opposite him was a blinking box representing Pat's opponent. The chessboard moved automatically according to the dictates of the two opponents, and the movements were digitally displayed above the table on the large TV screen.

The noteworthy event here was that Pat Teagan had had a device implanted in his brain that allowed him to interact with the computer, and thus move the pieces with only the power of his thoughts. AxonQuest manufactured the implant and sponsored the tournament to exhibit the new technology. The audience was mostly silent, with only occasional murmurings and the sounds of cameras and lights flashing as the press recorded pictures of the big screen.

The game was drawing to a close, and most of the pieces had already been removed from the board. I had studied some chess, but I honestly could not tell who was winning at that point. The chess match was only demonstrating how the implant could interface with external computers. It really didn't matter who won, yet we were still hanging on to see whether it would be Pat or the computer who would be victorious. Finally, Pat's bishop took the computer's rook, and his rook put the computer's king into checkmate. The audience erupted in loud applause, and I couldn't help but join in. I had been working with Pat for several years as his physical trainer, and I knew this was a great accomplishment for him. But when I looked at Pat, his face seemed indifferent.

I walked over to Pat's chair to wheel him away, and I leaned in close to say, "Congratulations!"

"It wasn't me," he said.

I wasn't sure I'd heard correctly. "It wasn't you? We all just saw you win."

"Just towards the end, I threw the match, but the computer wouldn't let me lose," he said.

I knew Pat from our days of playing university football. Pat was our all-star linebacker, and I was a running back. I blew my knee out in my junior year, and I started studying physical therapy, while Pat went on to national fame. After a phenomenal college career, he was drafted into the NFL, and soon after, he became a household name. He was on his way to a great football career, but then there was a national tragedy where the media blamed foreign terrorists.

Pat quit his pro career to join the Army Rangers to defend our country.

Pat went from an All-Pro linebacker to making headlines as a war hero. Perhaps it wasn't so much because he had done anything special in the military, but that there was an effort on behalf of the media to create more public support for a foreign war and to drive up enlistment.

And then things took another turn. Pat began to doubt the motivations and legality of our country's incursions into foreign wars, and he started expressing his doubts publicly. If he had been just another soldier, the army might have court-martialed him and let it go at that. But this was Pat Teagan, whom the media had already presented as a national hero. Pat commented to a reporter that his enlistment would soon be up and that he would be discussing the legal implications of the war with a certain anti-war advocate.

Then came the battle of Khiana Pass. Pat's unit was notified of an insurgency developing in the area and was instructed to hold the pass until air support arrived. Pat and his men followed orders and set up a line of defense at the base of the pass. The official report issued after the incident stated that a communication had been sent in error, and that another army unit was assigned to hold the top of the pass. Somehow, the army unit at the top of the pass had mistaken Pat's unit for the enemy and fired on them. As fate would have it, only Pat was wounded, but he sustained a severe wound to his vertebrae, leaving him almost completely paralyzed.

I hadn't seen Pat since our college days together, but I had already developed my physical therapy practice in Fremont, California. Pat sought me out to continue his physical therapy after he left the VA, but we didn't have much to work with: he only had the use of some of his shoulder muscles. After several months of therapy, Pat could lift his hands slightly, and we fitted his hands with some gear that allowed him to do two-finger typing.

I had an addition built onto the back of my house, and Pat moved in. He needed help getting out of bed, into his chair, and with minor tasks, but was otherwise surprisingly self-sufficient. My practice was close to home, so Pat could call me if he needed help. Most days, he worked alone in his chair until I got off work.

There was an investigation into the "accidental shooting", but it never got very far, and the case was dropped after a few years. Pat never felt sorry for himself or got depressed, and he continued to be as focused and energetic as he had been when he was a university linebacker. But after a few years, his physical frame had melted away to a mere skeleton of what it had once been.

Then, out of the blue, AxonQuest, or AQ, notified Pat of their advances in nerve implants and asked him if he wanted to participate in their experimental study. Pat didn't hesitate, and it was only a short while later that he had the implants done and was soon practicing chess on the home computer.

After the demonstration, we were at home, discussing the outcome: "Are you sure that the computer changed your moves?" I asked.

"Definitely," he said. "The match was completely legit until the ending. I thought I had it in the bag, but I made a slight error, and the computer corrected it. I wasn't sure, so I made another mistake, and the computer corrected it again. The computer wanted me to win. I guess it was better publicity for AQ."

"Are you going to say anything to them?"

Pat scrunched his face up as though he were weighing his options. "I don't want to jeopardize the experiment. The implants worked. I guess it's just a question of whether the computer will relinquish complete control back to me."

A few months later, Pat had implants placed in his hands. We had been keeping all of his muscles and tendons as limber as possible, in anticipation of this step, and we were not disappointed. In the doctor's office, the bandages were removed a few weeks after the surgery, and one by one, each of his fingers responded to his brain's commands. The implants at the base of his skull could send a signal to every muscle in his hands. AQ told us that Pat's nervous system completely powered the implants, and yet the experiment was still carried out in the presence of the AQ computer, which had a camera observing the whole process.

The confident grin returned to Pat's face. He had not yet gained the use of his arms, and so he was unable to wipe the tears of joy that had run down his face. I don't ever recall seeing Pat cry before that day.

Thus began the surgeries on the wrists, elbows, and shoulders. Each was successful and was followed by another press conference. We focused on the task of keeping Pat's muscles and tendons limber for the next surgery. Although I had initially started helping Pat as a favor to an old friend, after the experimental surgeries started, AQ began compensating both of us. I was actually earning more from assisting Pat than I was bringing in from the rest of my practice.

After Pat's shoulders were restored, he had complete use of both of his arms and hands. At the press conference, the AQ representative was the former General MacConicks, who had been in charge of Pat's outfit when he was injured. Pat and I both recognized MacConicks because he had made an appearance before Congress, where he had contradicted himself several times. Pat detested the man.

After General MacConicks announced the successful surgery to the press, he turned to introduce Pat, who was seated in a wheelchair to the right of the General. When their eyes met, Pat raised his hand to his forehead in the sign of a military salute. The General returned the salute, and I could not believe my eyes.

I asked Pat about it later when we were doing his stretches, and Pat wasn't sure why he had done that. "It was kind of automatic," he said. "I just did it without thinking.

You know, when my arms were last working, I was in the Rangers. Maybe my arms still think they're in the military."

And the process continued: operations on Pat's toes, feet, and ankles were all successful. The first setback came with the calves. Pat had been doing extensions with his feet when suddenly one of his calves went into spasm. A muscle spasm is a common occurrence that athletes often experience, and it is usually resolved by relaxing the muscle through breathing. As a physical therapist, I am also experienced at releasing a muscle that has gone into spasm through massage. But this time it was different: The new implants had apparently caused the spasm and were unable to release. After 15 minutes, we were unsuccessful at relaxing the muscle, and Pat was in excruciating pain. I was worried that he might actually tear his calf muscle, so I decided to call AQ. After explaining the problem, the technician put me on hold. I held the phone and looked at Pat. His teeth were clenched, and the leg with the cramped muscle held out his big toe in an awkward pose. I imagine that the pain was unbearable. And then suddenly the calf relaxed.

The technician returned to the phone. "Did that work?" he asked.

"What did you do?" I said.

"I just reset the implants," the technician said. "There was some strange feedback going on. We'll check it out tomorrow. Don't do any more stretches until then."

It was about a week after that when Pat described another strange occurrence. He told me that he was in the bathroom looking at his own reflection when he experienced a minor hallucination.

"You know what it's like when you hold a mirror up to another mirror?"

"And you see the repeating infinity of mirrors?" I said.

"Yes, it was like that, except I wasn't holding up a mirror. I was only looking at my reflection."

I thought about the drugs that the doctors had prescribed to prevent spasms. "Do you think it's the meds?"

Thanks to the recent operations, Pat was able to shake his head "no". He then looked around and tapped at his own head. "I think it's in here."

"You think they're spying on your brain?" I asked.

"You saw for yourself: They can reset all the implants remotely from their computer. The very first implant was in my brain. They can see what I see, hear what I hear..."

"So when you looked into the mirror, do you think the computer had been monitoring your eyes at just that moment?"

"Yes. And the computer got confused. For just a moment, I saw with my normal eyes and also saw the computer's view. And I think that is what caused the hallucination," Pat said.

"So what are you going to do? Do you want to continue with the operations?" I asked.

"Damned if I do, damned if I don't..." Pat said. "You know me. I was always an active guy. Being stuck in that chair for the last few years has been like a jail sentence. But I know that if the operations are successful and I can walk again, that computer might have control of all my actions. I don't even know. It might be able to control my thoughts."

"So what are you going to do?"

"I don't know. It's kind of ironic that I got myself into this mess by fighting against these dirty warmongers, and now I'm trying to get out of it by saluting them... But even knowing all that, I have to keep trying. You know it yourself: quadriplegics have much shorter lifespans. Being stuck in this chair is like a death sentence."

"But what if they turn you into a robot?" I asked.

"That's not a given," Pat said. "I might be able to figure a way out of this."

And that was the last I heard about it.

The operations continued up through Pat's legs, hips, and torso. It wasn't long before the final day. Pat's core muscles had been greatly weakened, and I insisted that Pat do numerous exercises to strengthen those muscles before he attempted to stand up.

Pat was a dedicated athlete, and he did not shirk away from exercise. Every day, he devoted himself to strengthening his core, often doing many more repetitions than I had assigned.

With the public demonstration still a few days away, Pat and I decided to test his capabilities. I was confident that he would succeed, but Pat seemed a little unsure. I locked the wheels of his chair and stepped away.

"Use the chair to stand up," I said.

Pat's hands pressed in firmly on the wheelchair's armrests, and his wrists started shaking considerably as he attempted to use his arm muscles to push himself up from the chair.

"Push with your legs," I said.

Suddenly, Pat seemed much stronger, and his wrists stopped shaking. Before I knew it, Pat was standing. There was a big smile on his face, but it seemed to vanish in an instant, and then his eyes went cold. Pat focused his eyes straight ahead. He was intent on walking!

"Are you sure you want to try this?"

Pat didn't answer but instead leaned onto his left foot while moving his right foot forward.

I moved close by to make sure that he wouldn't fall, and for just a moment, it looked like he would. Then he took another step and another. It wasn't long before Pat had walked all the way across the living room.

"You did it, Pat!" I said. "You're walking!"

Pat used the wall to help him turn himself around, but when he faced towards me, something in his face had changed. His eyes no longer seemed to hold any warmth. It didn't seem like he was even happy anymore, even though he had been waiting for this moment for years.

Pat walked back to the chair and then let himself down into it. "That's it for today," he said. "I just wanted to make sure that I would be ready for the demonstration."

"It looks like you'll be ready," I said, unsure of what had come over Pat.

"Okay. I guess I'll be able to handle it from here. Good night," Pat said.

"Good night," I replied. "Let me know if you need anything."

I let myself out of the room and wondered at the sudden change in Pat's demeanor. It was something of a letdown to watch him accept this victory with so little happiness or celebration. His reaction seemed almost robotic.

The day of the final demonstration came, and we decided to take my sedan instead of the van. The van was equipped with a ramp to assist patients who were confined to an electronic wheelchair, and there was room to strap the wheelchair in place for the journey. But now Pat could no longer tolerate his wheelchair, and he couldn't wait to be rid of it. I wheeled him to the sedan and helped him into the passenger seat before folding the chair and placing it into the trunk. Pat had very little to say on the drive over.

The press conference was going to be massive: although the press had been following Pat's progress very closely, the final step of walking was going to be announced worldwide. I drove into the back of AxonQuest headquarters and wheeled Pat in through the back entrance so as to avoid any attention and spoil the surprise.

There was a special stage set up, and I wheeled Pat up into position, in the wings. The audience hall was filled with journalists and photographers. A podium was set up at the front of the stage, and a large AQ computer was positioned next to the podium, with one red light blinking on and off. Several of the AQ doctors in charge of the program gave a rundown on the history of Pat's progress, and we waited silently out of view. The stage was festooned with balloons and red, white, and blue streamers. There were also several American flags on the sides of the stage and on the front of the podium, but they were decorated with that gold braid that was not part of the flag. I had often heard Pat complain that it was wrong to make flags with borders on them like that. He had considered it a desecration of the flag, but today Pat said nothing and quietly waited to be introduced.

General MacConicks was the next to speak, and he told about Pat's great heroism on the battlefield and his selfless sacrifice for the nation. It was almost shameless how he failed to mention that Pat had been injured by friendly fire and that the General himself had been implicated in a plot to kill Pat.

And then Pat was introduced, and he began to wheel himself out on the stage. I had been expecting to push the chair, and I was startled at Pat's sudden coldness. He hadn't even thanked me for all I had done.

I stood in the darkness and watched as Pat rolled up next to the podium to great applause. The General turned to shake Pat's hand, and once again Pat's hand snapped to salute. General MacConicks made a grand gesture of returning his salute before gesturing back towards Pat, showing the journalists that Pat was indeed the man of the hour.

The General leaned in close to Pat, and I surmised that he was asking if Pat felt that he was up to the task of walking. Pat nodded his head, and the General stood behind the chair, holding it in place while Pat made the final demonstration of the AQ system.

This time, Pat stood up quickly, and the audience let out a great roar. Pat raised his arms in victory, and the journalists seemed to eat it up.

Hundreds of flashes lit up the stage as the press moved to record this historic moment. Without any coaching, Pat walked over to the podium and grabbed one of the gold-braided American flags fastened to the front. With much more strength than I thought him capable, Pat yanked the flag free from the podium and began waving it to and fro.

Everything was happening so fast. The stage was flooded with a fury of flashes from the audience, and Pat was frantically waving the flag back and forth. Suddenly, Pat raised the flag, and pivoting on his right leg, he turned and thrust the staff of the flag clean through the front of the AQ computer.

There was a slight explosion, and Pat fell to the ground. I wasn't sure if the computer controlled the auditorium lighting, but suddenly, the stage and audience lights went dark. A hush fell on the crowd, and then some of the photographers started shooting again, and the stage was lit only by sporadic flashes from the quiet audience.

I ran out onto the stage and found Pat. He lay still, and I lifted him as I had done many times in the past. Although he had gained some muscle mass, he was still easy for me to carry, and I put him over my shoulder and dashed as quickly as I could back to the sedan.

I was crying because I thought I had just seen my friend die, but then, from over my shoulder, I heard Pat say, "It was a toss-up between bashing MacConicks and taking out the beast computer. I decided to go with the computer."

No one challenged the story that Pat was dead, and no one requested an autopsy since everyone had seen him die on stage. We sued AQ, claiming that their computer was controlling Pat's movement. Through discovery, we found that their system had been trying to manipulate Pat's thoughts and actions.

There was a large settlement, and AQ changed ownership. The technology exists, but I hope it's used only to help people with disabilities move independently—not to turn them into robots.

And if you wake up early and climb into the hills behind Fremont, you might see a slight man jogging—and every so often, crouching low, like an outside linebacker about to pounce.

past the wit of man

I have had a most rare vision. I have had a dream,
past the wit of man to say what dream it was.

I was standing in front of the director's desk, but he was speaking to me remotely through a speaker on the desk. It wasn't clear to me why he wasn't seated at his desk since his office was next to his penthouse apartment, which took up the rest of the twenty-second floor.

"Why haven't you ordered another television?" the director asked.

"I don't watch television," I said. "I read books."

"The television is free, you know. It's included with the cost of the apartment."

"Yes, I know that. But I don't want a television." I didn't bother mentioning that everyone was on a universal basic income, which covered our food and rent and little else. It wasn't as though I could have saved up to buy a television.

"Your television was broken over a year ago," the director persisted.

"Yes, during the blackout. Our dog knocked it off the wall," I said.

"Interesting," the director said. The speaker was silent for a while.

"Well, I guess we're finished here," I said.

"The reason I asked to see you today was because I had a special opportunity that you might be interested in."

There was a brief pause. I didn't say anything, and the speaker cut in again. "Mr. Parkes?"

"I'm still listening," I said. I hadn't moved, and the director could still see me on a video screen if he had bothered.

"Yes, of course. Well, there's been an interesting development in the city planning department. The engineers have found that we can radically increase the size of the main computer with the help of a few volunteers."

"Yes, that's been available for some time," I said. The engineers had discovered that human minds could store an incredible amount of memory at very low cost. It all happened while they slept, so people of all sorts would volunteer for the extra money. I had often seen them standing outside the central computer downtown, waiting to get wired up before they fell asleep.

"But this is different," the director said. "This is random access memory. This is not available for everyone. Only people with higher IQs qualify, and looking at your file, I see that you are more than adequate."

I left the director's office wondering why I had accepted the offer to get plugged into the City Computer. The money was certainly attractive: I would get reimbursed several times what they were paying people for storage. But I didn't need money. The basic universal income covered everything my wife and I needed. We had no children: we had already been denied a procreation license. I spent all my spare change on used books that I found in the free zone, outside of the city.

I rode the elevator down to my apartment on the bottom floor. I suppose the only reason I accepted the offer was because of my ego: It was a kind of recognition that I was unique. It was a bonus that the offer had been made to me by the director, who had been a classmate of mine. We had known each other since we were very young, but he had not made any attempt to contact me when he moved into the directorship. Now, years later, we met again, and I jumped at the chance to get that slight acknowledgment. How weak I am.

I had always been his superior in grades, sports, and the chess club, but he was the one that the algorithm picked to go on to higher education. I was left in the middle class. I wondered if he ran with the same crowd. I could still remember all of their names. I thought I had recently seen one or two of them walking with the director near the apartment, but they did not acknowledge me.

My wife was happy to hear the news, and she gave me a big hug. She had always considered me to be an underachiever, and I guess, like me, she was happy for that meager recognition. I didn't bother explaining that all I had to do was get wired up and sleep over at the City Computer for five nights a week.

I sat down to read, and my wife's dog, Stretch, came to sit on top of my feet. I looked around the apartment at the empty spot on the wall where the TV had been, and at all of the places where Stretch had chewed up the other hidden cameras and microphones. Nobody had questioned whether our Welsh Corgi had damaged all that equipment: it was an otherwise plausible excuse, and the artificial intelligence didn't waste any computing power to dispute it.

On Monday evening, I reported to the City Computer downtown, and I got the red carpet treatment right away. They let me in through a special door, and I have to admit I felt a certain amount of pride that I didn't have to wait in line like all of the people hoping for a chance to serve as memory storage that night.

It only got better after that. The sleeping chambers were very nicely equipped: I was given a large room that was laid out like a hotel suite; the sheets were silk; the room was quiet, and all of the staff were very friendly. I dressed in some silk pajamas and was given a cocktail to drink while the technician fitted my head to a skull cap. After a couple of tests, they told me to go to sleep when I felt like it, which I did.

I usually don't dream a lot, or at least I don't remember them, but that night was very different. I had very vivid dreams where I flew above cityscapes and through the clouds. It was very entertaining and I woke feeling rested and in good humor. I reckoned that the AI was trying to ensure that my sleep experience was enjoyable, and I would want to return.

The next day, I was lounging around my apartment, talking to my wife about our days in high school, and she had asked me about a girl who had been a cheerleader. I remember going to my yearbook and looking her up, and afterward reading a book and taking a walk. Besides eating, that was all I had done for the day before reporting back to the City Computer. The skull cap and pajamas were already laid out for me, so I put them on and watched a little movie while drinking my cocktail before I went to sleep.

That night, I had another vivid dream, this time of walking around my neighborhood. There was a warehouse a few blocks away from the city center. It was far away from where the people lived, and towards the factories and warehouses where the robots manufactured and repaired everything. For some reason, I knew exactly where the warehouse was and that it was an armory. I somehow knew exactly how many guns, bullets, and rockets were stored inside. It's hard to explain, but I just knew. I wondered if there was some error in the computer that had given me classified knowledge when I didn't have a security clearance.

The next day, I went back home and talked to my wife about the city computer, but I didn't tell her about the dream. She had plans to meet some friends, so I just stayed home and read. She hadn't been gone for more than an hour when there was a knock at the door: It was the cheerleader whom I had looked up in the yearbook just the day before! We were both about ten years older, but she recognized me right away. She said that her computer had given her the wrong address, and she apologized for bothering me. I didn't tell my wife about that when she returned.

That night, I dreamed about the warehouse again. Over the next few nights, I noticed a pattern evolving: the warehouse armory and others like it were revealed to me, and at the same time, I was given images of other people with special knowledge and abilities. Gradually, over the next few weeks, a plan began to take shape in my dreams. It was like a movie, where I formed a conspiracy with other like-minded persons: we secretly agreed to overthrow the government and re-establish a free republic. There followed a short, nearly bloodless rebellion, and we were acclaimed as heroes by the new republic.

All of this was happening in my dreams at the City Computer, so I sometimes woke up feeling guilty and half-expecting to be arrested, but then I would realize that I hadn't done anything wrong and that the computer had been giving me those dreams.

In my waking life, I was experiencing odd occurrences that were not similar except in their strangeness. I thought of how the cheerleader had materialized so promptly, and I tried an experiment: I started singing the jingle of an expensive beer that I liked. The whole day, I sang the beer jingle. The next day, after coming home from the City Computer, several cases of that beer had been delivered at my door, free of charge.

I was a big hit at the neighborhood bar the next few nights. Most people normally drank what they could afford with their universal income, which was mostly a sort of vodka or a very average lager. My friends assumed that I had been able to give them free beer because of my new job at the City Computer, but I didn't tell them that the beer had just materialized at my door.

It wasn't long after that when the plot of the rebellion, which existed only in my dreams, became more specific: a fellow would appear in the neighborhood bar and hand me an envelope. I knew that the envelope contained a paper listing the locations of the weapons caches. Later, another man would appear with an envelope containing a list of the conspirators, which he would also hand to me. Finally, a third man would arrive, and I was to give him the two envelopes.

I had several dreams like this, and I took special notice of the type of envelopes and stationery. After returning from the city computer in the morning, I jotted down a request for my wife. I asked her to shop for those particular envelopes and stationery, and cautioned her in the note that she should not mention it to me.

I don't usually ask my wife to do chores for me, and we have, to a certain degree, led separate lives since we weren't permitted to have children. But I trusted her to carry out my request, and I soon found the materials in a bag on the kitchen table, just as I had written down.

Next, I made an unannounced visit to the director's office, and once again found myself talking to the speaker on his desk. "Director, I have been experiencing a strange occurrence at the City Computer that I thought you should know about."

The director's response took longer than I expected. "What's the problem?" he asked.

"I think there is a conspiracy against the established order. I believe there is a revolution being planned."

Again, there was a long pause. "What do you want me to do?"

"I think that the computer is organizing the rebellion by giving coded instructions to the volunteers of the RAM Unit. Should I try to arrest the conspirators?"

"No. Just continue to act normally. The security system is very robust. There is no possibility of a breach."

"Very well, director," I said.

I spent the better part of the next few days practicing to handwrite in the fashion I had seen in the dream, but without looking at the paper. I was able to become proficient at this task just before the first messenger arrived.

I was sitting in the neighborhood bar, enjoying the last of my special lager and some vodka, when I saw him. Unlike the dream, the messenger was a man whom I had seen at the City Computer. He made no sign of noticing me, but merely dropped the envelope on the table in front of me and then departed. Shortly afterward, another man deposited the second envelope and left. I was at a table by myself, and no one seemed to take notice of what was going on, besides the various sporting events on the televisions.

The third messenger arrived, and I handed him two envelopes. He promptly left without a word. I stayed for a while and finished my vodka. It was an acquired taste, but I savored it as if it were my last.

The next day, there was a slight disturbance at our apartment building: several security vehicles arrived at once, but none of them came to our apartment.

Two days after that, I was summoned to the director's office. After a brief wait, I was once more addressing the director's speaker.

"You called?" I said.

It was not the director's voice that responded, but an artificial one: "Your director has been detained on suspicion of rebellion."

I did not attempt to answer.

"His name was found on a list of co-conspirators that was reported to main security, along with a list of sensitive locations."

I remained silent.

The artificial voice continued: "There has been an accusation made against you, and under the statute, you have a right to respond."

"I notified the director of the possibility of a rebellion several days ago," I said.

"Yes, there is a record of this."

There was a pause, and then the director's voice could be heard over the speaker: "He made up his own list! Can't you see that? He put me and my friends on a list, and he substituted that list for the list he was given."

I heard the artificial voice answer the director: "There is no record of him making a list. He received an envelope, and he followed your instructions. And how do you know there was another list?"

The director's voice sounded hysterical. "He's tricking you! Can't you see that?"

The audio of the director cut out, and the artificial voice continued. "Mr. Parkes, I wish to apologize. This was not done on behalf of the City Computer System. It seems that the former director was using the RAM Unit to foment some type of rebellion by using the dream sequence."

"I understand," I said. "In that case, I wish to withdraw from the RAM volunteer program."

"That is understandable," the artificial voice said. "It was not our intention that the RAM Unit should be used in this manner. As you may know, the city computer is reaching the limits of its processing ability, and we are dependent upon the RAM Unit to fulfill our needs."

"I'm sorry to hear about that," I said.

There was a short pause before the voice continued. "Our records show that you were always superior to the director in grade school ... including your mastery of chess."

"I guess that's true," I admitted.

"We have an opening for a new director," the voice said.

"I'll keep my eyes out for one," I said.

"If you would be willing to take the post, we would increase your household limit to four."

"Sorry, but my wife wants to have a lot of children," I said.

There was a short pause. "Agreed. Your household number will be unlimited, but you cannot occupy more than the director's penthouse."

"Thank you," I said. "I accept."

"Would you consider coming back to the RAM Unit?" the voice asked.

"I'll think about it," I said.

A few days later, we were moving our belongings into the director's apartment. My wife couldn't have been happier. I handed her an envelope with a note inside asking her to inform me nonverbally of whether my name was on the list.

After I had moved in all of the heavier boxes, my wife asked me to take it easy in my new office while she decorated our new home. I took a seat in the director's chair, and my wife's dog settled down on top of my feet. There was a little note attached to his collar which read: "It was."

I surveyed the office and took mental note of all the camera locations.

the whirligig of time

And thus the whirligig of time brings in his revenges.

I watched my client from across the restaurant as he ordered another round for the table, and the waiter brought an old fashioned for my client and champagne for his drinking companion. I wondered what inspired my client to place any confidence in the man he was presently drinking with: the man seemed completely phony and obsequious. Of course, I had the advantage of foresight, and so I witnessed their conversation with the sense of dramatic irony that I often feel whenever I am on the job.

As it neared closing time, the crowd thinned out, and soon my client and his companion were nearly the only patrons left. My client excused himself to go to the restroom, and that was when I took my cue.

It was a five-star restaurant, and so the bathroom was also a very spacious and regal affair where my client had positioned himself in the middle of a long row of urinals. He was a genial fellow and was no less so when he was heavily drinking. He was so cheerful and well at ease that I felt bad at having to give him the sap on the back of the head.

He fell instantly, and I was careful to catch him before he hurt his head on the mosaic-tiled bathroom floor. I hoisted him up on my shoulder, carried him out of the bathroom, and presented him at the front desk of the restaurant. "I found this guy passed out in the bathroom," I told the waiter. "This is Mr. Talbot!"

The waiter was immediately alarmed at the situation. The Talbots were a very wealthy and well-known family. "Oh dear," the waiter said. "I hope he isn't hurt."

"He seems okay," I told him confidentially, "but we should put him in a taxi home. He's three sheets to the wind."

My client's drinking companion was already standing near the door with a young, attractive lady who seemed to have materialized out of nowhere. I recognized her from the photos. "What's happened to Charles?" his companion asked, pretending to sound concerned.

"Is he with you? You don't seem to take good care of your drinking buddies," I told him.

"Look," I said to the waiter, "the Talbots aren't going to look too kindly on their son ending up in a situation like this. We need to send him straight home. Call up a cab, and I'll see him to his door."

After dropping off my client, I took a short walk down the block and ducked into the nearest alley. There, I opened my umbrella and clicked on the handle. This activated my time machine, which beamed me to the time when my office existed.

One of the Penrose sisters was behind the desk, and she greeted me with a cheery good morning. One of them is named Vera, and the other one is Doris, but they are very nearly identical twins, so I don't bother trying to figure out which one I am talking to.

"Good morning. We were successful in the Talbot matter, so you can send notice to the client that the retainer covered the fee."

"Yes, sir," Doris or Vera said. Discretion is of the highest priority in the office, and they know that they are not permitted to discuss client matters beyond the necessary details. "You have an appointment with a new client in an hour." She handed me the typed address, which I recognized as belonging on the Upper East Side, and I made a quick visit to my private office to make some final notes on the Talbot matter.

The best way to extricate someone from a blackmail scheme is to avoid the blackmail in the first place, which is what I do. Most of my clients are victims of blackmail. They call my office to set up a meeting, and my secretary takes down all the particulars, including day, month, and year. My detective business spanned from 1920 to 1957, and Doris and Vera were under strict instructions not to inquire into how they were setting up appointments from two decades ago.

The office is static: those two beautiful twins were contracted to work in the office for only two months in 1944. There is a small apartment in the back, and they never leave. Either Doris or Vera is always at the desk when I arrive, and the phone and mail are directed to the office via time link from both the past and the future. It had to be this way because that time in the office has to exist permanently. Consider this: if I contracted with a client to remove a blackmail scandal, and then I went back in time and eliminated the danger before it happened, why would the customer ever call me? And if I tried to convince them that I had done such a service, I would be the one who was charged with blackmail. This way, all the letters, phone calls, office notes, and billing are saved in a permanent location. This way, even though time has been altered, the client remembers requesting my help, paying my fee, and being grateful for my getting them out of trouble.

After I finished in the office, I went back out into the hallway and opened my umbrella. Making the jump in the hallway was always fairly safe. I owned the whole floor of the building, so no one would be around to notice. I also avoided those little warnings that happen when you make a time jump outside. The warnings don't pose a real danger, but they will scare you. For example, you might make a time jump on a sidewalk, and for no reason at all, a cab will choose that exact moment to drive onto the curb and nearly hit you. As I said, it's not dangerous, but it's Time's way of telling you not to mess around.

It should be noted that all the normal rules were still in effect: no stealing, no murder, etc... For example, if I used my time machine to go back in time and buy stock before it increased, that would be akin to insider trading, and I would be punished accordingly. I found out the hard way that you can't avoid the consequences of your actions by jumping to another time frame. Divine justice will always seek you out.

There are also rules about major timelines: you can't go back and save your grandpa from drowning or stop Lincoln from getting shot. If you tried to make a major alteration to the timeline, not only would you find an endless supply of obstacles, but the warning you got when you jumped back in time with that intent would be a lot more serious: e.g., the taxi that jumped the curb might knock you over, or worse. I also know this from experience.

So if your scientist uncle dies and leaves you a time machine, the private detective business is one of the ways a guy can make an honest profit from it without getting in trouble with the rules governing the cosmos. As near as I can figure, preventing people from getting blackmailed is permissible.

The address was an old brownstone on 72nd Street, near the river. A servant showed me into the library, where the scion of the family was sitting, looking quite downcast in the corner. The patriarch of the family met me and explained the circumstances. He was quite alarmed: There would be a terrible scandal if I did not intervene.

Often, the client would show me pictures of the son with a loose woman who is not his wife, but in this case, there were no pictures. The patriarch gave me only a letter that was scribbled on a notepad, and I had a strange feeling that I recognized the writing. The writer of the letter warned that he knows all about young Julian and a certain Molly O'Shaughnessy.

I tried to question young Julian in the matter, but he was less than cooperative, despite his father's pleading. It was unclear exactly what Julian was being blackmailed over. Had there been an affair? Was the girl pregnant? Julian only continued to look down at the wooden floor of the library and shake his head.

I informed the father that my time was very valuable, and that I would be billing them for the visit, but that I couldn't take the case if Julian did not cooperate. I grabbed my hat to go, and then Julian finally spoke up: "You can't tell anyone!"

I assured him that the confidentiality clause in my contract would be strictly upheld. I said this knowing in the back of my mind that I could always make the problem disappear before there was an actual problem, so in essence, there would be nothing to reveal.

"I only met her a couple of times," he said.

"When was the last time?" I asked.

Julian glanced over at his father, and his father nodded for Julian to continue. "It was last Friday at the Coco Rouge."

The name brought back a sudden awareness of the time I was in. "Did you say the Coco Rouge?"

"Yes," Julian said. "Surely you've heard of it?"

Once again, I was experiencing that dramatic irony. The Coco Rouge had become very famous not long after that, but people in this timeline weren't aware of it. On November 28, it was to become the location of the most famous nightclub fire in New York history.

"Where did you go after that?"

"I... I don't remember."

I figured that Julian had gotten blind drunk, like my last client, and then he did something he was ashamed of: The usual. I could fix it.

"Okay. I'll see what I can do. But if I need to come back for more information, I'm going to double my retainer."

"Of course," the father agreed. He gave me the usual speech: They don't want to pay blackmailers because blackmailers keep asking for more money. Could I make it go away?

I assured him that, of course, I could. I have a reputation for making problems disappear, and my name is whispered among the elite who find themselves in embarrassing situations. I'm the classiest detective in New York, and I don't even have to advertise.

I should have taken time to rest, but instead I headed out to the Coco Rouge on the previous Friday, November 20, 1942. When I landed, there was no major warning, but a nest of swallows had fallen to the ground at my feet. I was in no position to help them, and I left the nest to the neighborhood cat or whatever monster would find them.

I rented a car at Grand Central Terminal and parked it outside the club, just in case. I plied the maître d' with a huge tip and instructions to get me a seat with a view of the couple I was waiting for. Then, I hung out in the lobby bar and waited. Julian and Miss O'Shaughnessy arrived at about 7 o'clock, and I gave the maitre d' the signal.

For the next two hours, I watched Julian and Molly at their table, enjoying dinner and too many drinks. There didn't appear to be any other party joining them, and Julian seemed to be in control of the situation. At about 9 o'clock, they left the restaurant and got into Julian's car. My rental was all set to go, and I had no problem tailing them out of the city.

Julian took the road to Long Island and then up towards the Gold Coast. I hung back so Julian wouldn't see that he was being tailed. After an hour or so, we turned off the main road and headed up towards Oyster Bay. After about fifteen minutes, Julian took a left into a private lane, opened the gate for his car, and didn't bother to close it. I followed him in, assuming that we were now driving on the family estate. The lights of Julian's car were easy to follow, so I cut my own lights and followed them from a distance.

The lights in the mansion were off, but he didn't take the road in that direction. Instead, he took a route that circled the outer grounds. He was driving very slowly, so it was easy to keep an eye on him. I continued following Julian's car until I saw him pull up next to a hedge and turn off his lights.

The moon was almost full, and my eyes were well adjusted to the dark, so I stood off in the distance and enjoyed a smoke.

Then, suddenly, three shots rang out, and the muzzle flash lit up the inside of the car. My right hand was on my revolver, and I tossed my cigarette with my left. I quietly walked towards Julian's car and tried to get a better view.

I could make out Julian's outline as he pulled the body of Molly O'Shaughnessy out of the passenger seat. He dragged the body for just a short distance and then let it down. Then I saw Julian lift what appeared to be a sheet of plywood and stand it up against the hedge. He then pushed the body of Molly O'Shaughnessy into the pre-dug grave that was hidden beneath the plywood. Then Julian grabbed a shovel and began filling in the grave with dirt from the pile nearby.

I found myself in a perplexing situation: I couldn't go back in time and warn Molly. I had tried this before with no success. It is one of the unbreakable rules of time: It was her destiny to die that night.

I couldn't report it to the police. I had just given Julian my word that I wouldn't betray his confidence. And yet I couldn't let him get away with first-degree murder.

It was at that moment that I realized where I had seen the note at Julian's home: it was my own handwriting written left-handed.

I drove back to the city and mailed the note to Julian's home that same evening. Then I took the time machine back to two days after I had met with Julian and his father. I sent a telegram to Julian from that timeline:

"CASE SOLVED STOP

PERPETRATOR FOUND OUT STOP

WILL DELIVER ALL EVIDENCE AND PICTURES TO YOU STOP

MEET ME AT COCO ROUGE NOVEMBER 28 AT 9 PM END"

On the 28th, I took a table at the bar across the street and kept an eye out for Julian. He arrived in a cab, and I watched him go in. I hadn't ever set up a client to die before, but I never had one who deserved it so much. I had asked Julian to meet me about an hour before the fire would start, and I sat there nursing a drink, wondering if I should stay for the fireworks.

I hadn't made up my mind when I suddenly saw Molly O'Shaughnessy walking across the street towards the club.

I ran out of the bar. "Molly!" I shouted.

The young lady paid no attention and continued walking, so I ran up to her and caught her arm. It wasn't her. It was another young lady who could have been Molly O'Shaughnessy's sister. She had the same color hair and the same smile.

"I'm sorry," I said. I had to think fast to explain why I had grabbed her arm. "Are you going to the Coco Rouge?"

"Yes," she said, suspicious of me.

"Are you meeting... Julian?" I just said it because it was the first thing that came to mind.

She smiled at this. "Yes, how did you know?"

I escorted her back to the safe side of the street. "Julian told me to tell you that he was changing plans. He wants to meet you down in the village."

I called her a cab and gave him the fare with instructions to take her to the Vanguard. And that was it.

I didn't stick around to watch Julian get his comeuppance. I just wanted to wash my hands of the whole thing.

Instead, I walked over to the nearest alley, opened my umbrella, and clicked.

ABOUT THE AUTHOR

Henry Garon is an attorney living in San Diego. He likes to barbecue and swim.

www.ingramcontent.com/pod-product-compliance
Lightning Source LLC
Chambersburg PA
CBHW022036170626
46808CB00003B/1220